PRAISE FOR FRANK M. ROBINSON'S
LAST NOVEL, *WAITING*

"A Top-10 Book for the Summer"—NPR's "All Things Considered"

"*Waiting* can be best described as an anthropological thriller . . . with nice action sequences and fine writing. *Waiting* is not a simple rewrite of *The Power*. It's a different spin that offers loyal readers a glimpse of the author's intelligence and wit."

—*Mystery News*

"*Waiting* is a thriller with smarts, and it is a pleasure to recommend. Characters are richly detailed, and the plot twists are fascinating as well as credible in this very fine novel. Robinson creates terror in everyday settings—there is no safe harbor. *Waiting* is a novel of suspense that makes you think about the larger questions of illusion and reality. What happens to your sense of self and its place in the world when you learn that someone you've known all your life is nothing like you knew? . . . Read *Waiting* with all the lights on and all the doors and windows locked, not that mere locks and lights will save you."

—*Bay Area Reporter*

"Robinson's *Waiting* is not a sequel to the book that put him on the science fiction map, *The Power*, although it does connect to the earlier novel. Many readers regard *The Power* as the best book yet written about what a true superhuman being would be like, walking like an invisible god among men. . . . While this novel may not have the impact of *The Power*, it's a very good book and, the two together provide an unusual example of an interesting science fiction theme looked at from two different perspectives."

—*The Orlando Sentinel*

"A spellbinding novel by acclaimed master of suspense Frank Robinson."

—*Playboy*

"Jolting murders and mind-boggling spe~~~ ~~~   api-
ens coexist in this excellent book."

~~~st"

"Suppose another species of human   for
35,000 years, waiting to take over. ~~~   he
latest thriller by Frank M. Robinson

—*Chicago Tribune*

"A truly frightening and plausible story about another species of human beings, in hiding for 35,000 years and now ready to take control of the planet . . . Robinson grips his readers by combining visceral fear with intellectual inquiry. This creepily credible tale will have his readers looking more closely at their so-called friends."

—*Publishers Weekly* (starred review)

THE POWER

FRANK M. ROBINSON

TOR®

A TOM DOHERTY ASSOCIATES BOOK
NEW YORK

THE POWER

Book design by Lynn Newmark

A Tor Book

Published by Tom Doherty Associates, LLC
175 Fifth Avenue
New York, NY 10010

www.tor.com

Tor® is a registered trademark of Tom Doherty Associates, LLC.

ISBN 0-312-86654-2

First Tor Edition: March 2000

Printed in the United States of America

0 9 8 7 6 5 4 3 2 1

FOR THE MEMORY OF MY MOTHER
who liked a
good thriller

You remind me of a man.
What man?
The man with the power.
What power?
The power of hoo-doo.
Who do?
You do!
Do what?
Remind me of a man.
What man?
The man with the power . . .

THE POWER

1

OLSON was cracking up.

He had seen it coming for a whole month now, Tanner thought. Every day Olson had grown more nervous until now the psychologist reminded him of a fine crystal goblet—ping him just right and he would fly into a thousand pieces.

The others had noticed it, too, which meant that he would have to do something about it sooner than he had thought. And no matter how he sliced it, getting rid of Olson was going to be a dirty job. And then again, it might be possible to do something *for* Olson, though he didn't know what.

He paused for a moment in the doorway of the Science building and dug the bowl of his pipe into his tobacco pouch, forcing the grains of tobacco in with a heavy thumb.

What the hell was eating Olson?

He zippered the pouch shut, then took a last breath of spring air and pushed through the glass doors. The Project laboratories were already filling up with the usual influx of Saturday-morning students, eager to pick up a spare dollar. They flocked in and signed waivers and then the graduate assistants assigned them to the different experiments.

He stopped by the cold room for a moment to watch a volunteer floating in icy water, thin, threadlike wires leading to thermocouples strapped to various parts of his body. They would fish the man out before any damage had been done, he reflected, but then human beings were pretty durable; they could always stand more than they thought they could.

He stared for a while in silence, then walked down the white-washed corridor to the Limits Experimentation lab where Commander Nordlund was supposed to meet him.

Olson.

A pudgy young man, his own age, who hid behind a pair of thick, horn-rimmed glasses. Brilliant, narrow-minded, and antisocial. The kind for whom a university was always a refuge, but not the kind you expected to flip his wig, either. Something had happened to Olson—but just exactly what?

He would have to do something about it and the other members of the committee would watch him closely to see how he handled it. If he fumbled it . . . Well, Van Zandt had the hatchet out for him and would administer the *coup de grâce* with as much dispatch as possible; you probably wouldn't even see the blood. Tanner was chairman today, would he be flunky tomorrow?

In the Limits lab, Commander Arthur Nordlund was half sitting on a table, cigarette dangling from pale fingers, watching a pain experiment. Nordlund was waiting to talk to him about Olson, Tanner thought, and he couldn't blame the man for it—much as he might dislike Nordlund. There were eight people in the United States who knew the limits of human endurance better than anybody else on earth. The government couldn't afford to let any one of them slip his moorings and start to talk.

"How's the world going, Commander?"

Nordlund smiled faintly and managed to look annoyed at the same time. He was slender, the type that looked good in a uniform, with sharp, delicate features and a pencil-thin moustache. He was in his early thirties, not much older than Tanner.

But I can't talk to him, Tanner thought. *He's the silk type of personality and I'm the tweed, and never the twain shall meet.*

Nordlund pointed a well-manicured finger at the experiment going on in front of him. "What's the point, Professor?"

"We're measuring pain thresholds, seeing how much a man can take." He studied the young man strapped in the chair in front of him. He had been stripped down to his T shirt and pants, then a small, black circle painted on his forehead. A beam of intense, white light had been focused on the circle.

Tanner waved his hand and an assistant at a nearby control board inched a rheostat ahead another notch. The beam of light brightened and a fine halo of static electricity played over the figure in the chair. The man's hair abruptly stood out from his head in a sudden crackle of blue sparks and his face became greasy with sweat.

"Okay, cut it!" The whine of the generator died away and Tanner started to loosen the straps. "How do you feel?"

"I don't think I could have taken any more of that, Professor—it was really cutting me up!" The student wiped his face with his T shirt and turned to Nordlund. "Is the Navy really going to use the results of tests like this, sir?"

Tanner cut in before Nordlund could reply. "They're all necessary in survival research, Chuck." He clapped the boy on the shoulder. "Wash off the lampblack and you can beat it for the day."

After he had gone, Nordlund said, "Since you seem to know all the answers, Professor, mind telling me how that one worked?"

I rubbed him the wrong way. Again. I'm really an ace at getting along with the brass.

"It wasn't too difficult. The white light caused a pain reaction on the spot on his forehead. The static charge measured skin conductivity—it changes under pain conditions."

"How painful was it?"

"About as painful as it gets; almost as bad as the pain somebody has when they pass kidney stones."

"Is that the limit of how much a man can take?"

"Depends on the man. Football players can take more than poets, if you follow me."

Nordlund looked bored. "I could have told the government that myself."

"You mean you would have *suspected* it but you wouldn't have been sure. The government pays for proof." Tanner started for the door. "Ready?"

Nordlund didn't move. He flicked open a German cigarette lighter that lit on contact with the air. "Before we go in, don't you think we ought to discuss what you're going to do with Olson?"

"I was thinking of having a talk with him."

Nordlund shook his head. "Uh-uh. That won't wash, Professor, it's not enough. The man's in bad shape and I want to know what you're going to do about it and when."

He was going to hate to do it, Tanner thought slowly. Whatever was bothering Olson, firing him from the committee might be the straw that broke the camel's back.

Nordlund read his expression and a slight tinge of authority crept into his voice. "I appreciate your feelings for the individual in this case, Professor. But even though this isn't the hydrogen bomb project, it's still security work. The government can't afford to have a man go to pieces on work like this. It's like a line on board ship—when you see it's frayed and might snap, you replace it."

We must keep everything shipshape at all costs. To hell with Olson. And ten to one the bastard has never been on board ship. Aloud he said, "I'll tell him after the meeting. Maybe I can convince him he needs a rest, something like that."

Nordlund stood up. "Handle it any way you please. And while we're at it, what about his sister? She's never struck me as being a stable type, either."

Tanner turned on his heel. "It's a little late to shake up the whole committee, Commander."

"Suit yourself, Professor, I function only in an advisory capacity." His voice changed slightly and Tanner could almost feel the piano wires in it. "But if anything goes wrong, we'll know where the responsibility lies, won't we?"

They got to the seminar room just before the rest of the committee members arrived and Tanner settled back to study them as they filed in.

Patricia Olson—Petey, for short—his secretary and Olson's sister, was first. She might have been pretty but she wore no rouge or lipstick to dress up what she had. She wore her hair pulled back in a bun and plastic-framed glasses with perfectly round, enormous lenses that gave a tarsier-like expression to the slightly flat face behind them. A nose that could be called pert, a perpetual frown, and thick, unplucked eyebrows. Efficient. Calm. And very cold.

The next was Professor Owen Scott, whom campus mythology had built up as another Mr. Chips. A shell of a once-vigorous man, Tanner thought, with a wisp of tattletale gray hair hanging over a lined face. The chairman of Tanner's Anthropology Department but a little too old for chairmanship of the committee.

Marge Hanson of Biology came in giggling at some comment of the man behind her. Auburn haired, a larger and far prettier girl than Petey was, but like Petey, one who insisted on low-heeled shoes and sensible skirts. The type who played tennis and swam and danced all night and woke up early the next morning still thinking the world was a wonderful place to live in.

She caught his eye, said "Hi!" and winked. He caught himself smiling and winked solemnly back.

The wit who had made Marge laugh was Karl Grossman, Physics, a fat, untidy man who never tucked in his shirt securely enough. Then there was Eddy DeFalco, the third member of the Anthropology Department. Tanned, muscled, cocky, and confident.

The girls adore him, Tanner thought. *The boyish type they go to bed with when they're off on a vacation and nobody knows them. But why blame Eddy just because he's lucky?*

Professor Van Zandt, the head of the Psychology Department, was a thin, nervous man in his middle forties with ice-blue eyes that were unnaturally sharp. There was a little too much padding in his suit-coat shoulders and Tanner had a hunch that beneath the double-breasted coat there was the beginning of a slight paunch.

Beware the Ides of March, for Van will get me if I don't watch out. . . .

Bringing up the rear was John Olson, Petey's older brother, nervously moistening his thick lips and hanging on every word that Van Zandt was saying. He looked jumpy and scared.

Why?

They were all different, Tanner thought. And they all had their faults. But it was a good committee. It was probably one of the brainiest that could be assembled at any university in the United States. . . .

"If we're all here," Grossman grunted heavily, "why should we delay?"

Tanner nodded to Petey, who started to read the minutes of the last meeting. *"Saturday, May twenty-second. The meeting of the Navy Committee for Human Research was called to order . . ."*

Tanner waited until she had finished reading the minutes, then made a show of fumbling with his pipe, wondering briefly how many of them knew it was Young Man with Prop.

"During the last year," he started easily, "we've been doing primarily survival research—why some men live and some men die under different stresses and environments. Under battle conditions, certain men are smarter, more efficient, and more capable than others. Having determined the qualities necessary for survival, we've been trying to figure out how the successful ones, the ones who *do* survive, get that way, what factors play a part."

He champed a little harder on his pipe and squinted through the smoke. "Hunting for people with these characteristics has been a little like hunting for a needle in a haystack, so John Olson suggested a questionnaire—where you can cover a lot of people quickly at a small cost. Those who showed promise on the questionnaire could be given more exhaustive physical tests later. As you recall, the questionnaire we drew up covered an individual's past medical history, psychological outlook, family background, and heredity—all the items we had agreed were important, and many of which can hardly be tested in a physical sense anyway." He smiled cautiously. "We all agreed to take the test ourselves last week—sort of as a dry run. None of us signed our names, for which I'm sorry. John's compiled the results and I must admit there were some pretty fantastic answers on one of them."

DeFalco looked curious. "Like what?"

Tanner held up one of the questionnaires. "The person who filled it out, if we take it at face value, has never been sick, never had any serious personal problems, never worried, and has an IQ close to the limits of measurability. His parents came from two distinct racial stocks and for what it might be worth, his father was a water dowser and his mother a faith healer."

There was a ripple of laughter around the table and even Professor Scott was grinning. Tanner put the questionnaire aside. It had been good for a chuckle at least.

"If there are no more suggestions, I'll have Petey send the form to the printers, then . . ."

"Professor Tanner!"

He glanced down at the end of the table. Olson's pudgy face was covered with a light sheen of sweat that glistened in the sunlight coming through the windows.

"Do you think that questionnaire was on the level?"

Tanner felt annoyed. If Olson had had doubts about it, why hadn't he asked him about it in private, rather than bring it up now?

"You mean, did I fill it out as a gag? No, I didn't—but obviously somebody did."

Olson wet his lips again. "Are you so sure of that?"

There was an uneasy silence, then Professor Scott snorted, "Rubbish!"

Olson didn't give ground. "Maybe there's something to it. I think we ought to . . . look into it."

Nordlund edged into the conversation. "If it's on the level . . ."

"It isn't," Tanner said curtly.

"But if it was?"

One layman in the crowd and you spent the whole damned afternoon explaining the ABCs.

"If it was on the level it would mean the person who filled it out was a very unusual human being, perhaps a very superior one. But I hardly think we should take it seriously. And there are a lot of important things to cover today."

Olson's voice rose to a nervous squeak. "Maybe you don't want to admit what it means, Tanner!"

They were all staring at Olson now. His face was damp and his eyes a little too wide. The eyes of a man scared half to death, Tanner thought clinically. Then he could feel the sweat start on his own brow. He had a hunch that Olson was going to blow his stack right in the committee room.

He tried to head him off, to get the frightened man to talk it out. "All right, John, just what do you think it means?"

"I think it means the human race is all washed up!"

Tanner glanced over at the Navy man and could see that Olson's outburst was going over like a lead balloon with Nordlund; there was a look of shocked surprise on the other faces. A moment of embarrassed silence followed, then Petey, looking as if she were about to cry, said, "John, I think we better . . ."

Olson didn't look at her. "Shut up, Pat."

Nobody said anything. They were going to let him handle

it, Tanner thought uneasily. It was his baby. He held up the questionnaire. "Who filled this one out?"

Another strained silence, one where a slight, uneasy movement in a chair or an embarrassed fumbling with papers sounded very loud.

"Don't you think we ought to skip this?" Van Zandt said impatiently. "I don't see how it's getting us any place."

Tanner flushed. He was trying to humor Olson and Van Zandt knew it but then, this was the academic jungle. Van had won his spurs a long time ago, but he still liked to keep in practice.

He dropped the questionnaire. "All right, we'll forget it for now." He nodded to Olson. "See me after the meeting, John, and we'll talk about it then."

"You're scared!" Olson screamed in a hysterical voice. "You don't want to believe it!"

Tanner could feel the hair prickle at the back of his neck. Take the survival tests and couple them with an inferiority complex and maybe you ended up with a superman fetish. Something half akin to religion—a willingness and desire to believe in something greater than yourself. But why was Olson so frightened about it?

Olson was trembling. "Well? What are you going to do about it?"

It was like watching an automobile accident. It repelled you but you couldn't tear your eyes away. There was a sort of horrible fascination to this, too—the sight of a man going to pieces. He waited for Van Zandt to say something, to squelch his younger colleague with a few broadsides of logic. But Van said nothing and only stared at Olson with a curious, speculative look in his eyes. Nobody knew Olson better than Van Zandt, Tanner thought, but for reasons of his own, Van was letting John dig his own grave and wasn't going to argue him out of it.

He was sweating. There was nothing left to do but go along with Olson. He turned to Marge. "Do you have a pin?"

She found one in her purse and handed it over. He stood a

book on end on the table, embedding the head of the pin between the pages so the point projected out about an inch. Then he tore off a tiny fragment of newspaper, folded it into a small, umbrella shape, and placed it on the pin point.

"Maybe we can prove something this way, John. I'm assuming that our . . . superman . . . has mental powers such that he could make this paper revolve on the pin merely by concentrating on it. The paper is light, it's delicately balanced, and it wouldn't take much to move it. Okay?"

There was a round of snickers but Olson nodded and Tanner felt relieved. It was the only thing he could think of on the spur of the moment. A kid's game.

"Anybody care to try?"

Marge said, "I'm willing if everybody else is."

The others nodded and she stared intently at the pin. The paper hung there quietly, not stirring. After a minute she leaned back, holding her hands to her head. "All I'm doing is getting a headache."

"Van?"

Van Zandt nodded and glared at the paper umbrella. If sheer will power could do it, Tanner thought, Van Zandt was his man. But the paper didn't move. Van Zandt leered. "My superior talents apparently aren't in evidence this morning."

Olson himself and then DeFalco tried and failed. Nordlund stared intently at the pin and then looked bored when the paper didn't even tremble. It was Professor Scott's turn next.

The paper hat tilted slightly.

There was a thick, frightened silence. The condescending attitude had vanished like a snap of the fingers and Tanner could feel the tenseness gather in the room. All eyes were riveted on the suddenly trembling old man. *"My God, I didn't . . ."*

"Very simply explained," Grossman said quickly. "A door slammed down the hall, though I doubt that any of you heard it in your concentration. I am sure that a slight draft would be enough to affect our little piece of paper."

The old man looked enormously relieved and some of the tenseness drained away. Grossman tried it next, with no result.

Tanner shrugged. "Well, John?"

Olson was suddenly on his feet, leaning his knuckles on the table and glaring down the length of it. *"He* won't admit it, he hasn't got the guts! If he wouldn't admit he had filled out the questionnaire, he wouldn't show himself in a test like this!" His pudgy face was red. "He hasn't got the nerve, Tanner, he's hiding!"

What the hell do you do in a case like this? Tanner thought. They were babying a neurotic but they had gone this far and it wouldn't hurt to go a little further. He'd play along just once more. *I feel embarrassed for the poor guy. And it's partly my fault; I should have done something about it a week ago.*

"We'll try it again, only this time all together." Olson's superman could still hide and yet reveal his powers—if he wanted to take on Olson's dare. When nothing happened, maybe then John would be convinced. Except that you could never dissuade a neurotic when they wanted to believe in something. . . .

He nodded to the others.

On the street outside there were the faint sounds of automobile traffic and the muted vibrations of conversation. Some place far away tires screeched. Equally remote were the indignant complaints of a housewife, shortchanged at a sidewalk fruit stand. In the room itself, there were no sounds, not even the muffled sighs of breathing. And there was no motion, other than that of the small motes of dust floating in the bars of sunlight that streamed through the window.

And the tiny paper umbrella which trembled, tilted, and then spun madly.

2

TANNER stirred restlessly under the sheets, then reached for the window shade and pulled it aside slightly so he could see out. It was a miserable night. Dark clouds were scudding across the face of the moon and in a few minutes they'd probably start to seep rain. A little at first, and then the deluge would pound the sidewalk and shred the trees and the wind would bring down all the dead branches.

The street lamps lined the walk like king-size candles and a mile away he could see the red glow that marked the winking neon of Chicago's Howard Street. There was a bar down there that didn't catch any of the student trade and didn't go in for any of the shrieking jazz combos. It was there he usually took Marge when he was in a talkative mood. And where he wished he was now. . . .

The rising wind rattled the pane and whistled through the narrow space between window and frame. The cold air on his naked stomach made him shiver. Summer wasn't here yet after all, he thought. Or had it been just the chill air? Maybe it was the idea that the moon and the dark clouds were looking down on someone else right then—somebody who was as superior to him as he was to a moronic bushman.

He thought back to what had happened that morning. The paper umbrella had spun like a dervish and they had sat there, frozen with fear and amazement. His own self-confidence had left him with all the speed of a small boy sliding down a banister and his stomach had felt as if he had been eating chopped ice for breakfast. For a brief moment his world had wobbled and teetered and almost collapsed.

Then Grossman had sworn in guttural German and had hit the book with his open palm, crushing the paper hat and pin down among the pages. Then they had left, babbling to each other and with no immediate plans on what to do next.

Well, to hell with it.

He fumbled on the bed table and found his pipe and lit it. The bowl glowed dimly in the dark and the smoke took some of the chill off his chest. He lay back on the pillow and stared out the thin space between the shade and the window frame, looking at the speeding clouds and the winking stars without actually seeing them.

Why did some people live through wars and others not? No survival factors were concerned when you were killed outright, of course. There was little that could be done to stop a bullet or an exploding shell. But a lot of men died from . . . call it fringe factors. Stupidity was one. Mental instability was another.

A superior type wouldn't suffer from insanity, neurosis, or worry. It would be a type that could stand up under brainwashing. It would be physically strong and have quick reflexes. It wouldn't go to pieces quite so easily.

There were a thousand other survival factors. Good digestive systems, like most endomorphs were gifted with. A person who got more mileage out of his food, could get along on less, if he had to—a strong survival factor if food was hard to get. Resistance to disease and cancer would be another survival factor. And an ability to get along with people.

He bolstered his pillow and slid up on it, half sitting up in bed.

There were other survival factors, other talents that were hard to find in people and even harder to study. The whole vast field of abilities that most scientists didn't even care to talk about—or admit exist. There were people who knew what was going to happen a few moments before it actually did or what somebody was going to say a few seconds before he said it.

It had even happened to him once. It was during a raffle at church. He was on his feet and walking to the stage a full five seconds before Father Culligan, looking astonished and somewhat pained, called out his name. It had been embarrassing and not too easy to explain away. A lot of people still thought it was a put-up job.

And then there was the ability to move small objects through the power of the mind alone. He had seen it done that morning. At least *something* had whirled the tiny paper umbrella.

But there was still one thing that bothered him.

He had known everybody in that seminar room, well enough to call by the first name and to know the skeletons in the family closet. And he couldn't quite see any of them as being . . .

The better human being.

Next year's model.

The man to whom the world belonged.

He yawned and tapped his pipe on the window sill. A breeze caught the curtains and brought out the goose flesh again. And then it occurred to him. *My God, what a scientific study! The Man of Tomorrow—Today!*

He sat bolt upright. It *could* be the most wonderful thing

that had happened to the human race since the first ape had descended from the trees. A human being with suddenly increased capabilities that could be fed back genetically to improve the race as a whole. A man who could be studied and analyzed and the results applied to human behavior problems, a man who could take the human race by the hand and lead it upward. If he wanted to.

But why wouldn't he?

Olson.

Olson had been positive the man would hide. Olson had been insistent on some kind of a test. And Olson had been scared to death, scared enough to stand up against group disapproval, which had probably never happened before.

He suddenly regretted that he had never got to know Olson very well, that he had never gone out of his way to be friends with the man. Olson was the type who desperately needed friends and companionship, who needed to lean on other people. All in all, the faculty at the university had been cold to Olson—himself along with the others.

He looked at his watch. It wasn't too late in the evening. In fact, eleven o'clock Saturday night was ridiculously early.

He swung his legs over the side of the bed and walked to the phone, the cold air in the room sending chills over his naked body.

The familiar buzzing and then Susan Van Zandt's voice. *"Hello?"*

"Hello, Sue. John there?"

"Bill? No, he isn't in. Do you want me to have him call you?"

He hesitated. Olson must have gone out, though he had gotten the impression that John was just as tired as he was and had made no plans for the evening. Maybe a movie or something . . .

"Forget it, Sue. I'll call him tomorrow."

Olson not being home meant nothing at all, he decided, except that Saturday night, despite the weather, was too good a night to waste by sleeping.

He sat down on the phone table and dialed Marge's number.

* * *

"Waiting long?" Tanner asked.

"Long enough to order for both of us, and have two men try to pick me up. And I'm sure that the waitress thinks that anybody who orders Scotch-on-the-rocks and a glass of beer at the same time is a little odd."

He slid into the booth beside her. "You should have ordered two Scotches. Then the waitress would have considered you a common drunk and perfectly normal."

She made a face. "I like you better when you're not trying to be clever."

He drained half his beer and looked at Marge over the top of the glass. She wore her auburn hair in an Italian cut that went very well with her light coat of tan. She didn't fuss over clothes but she knew how to wear them. A plaid skirt and a light green sweater and a thin, choker necklace. A wisp of perfume and the faint odor of sweetly scented soap.

She was the pretty teacher, the type every freshman falls in love with.

"Stop it! You're looking at me as if I were a butterfly on a pin!"

"Not a really beautiful butterfly, Marge—but definitely a pretty one."

She wrinkled her nose. "You can think up a better line than that, Bill. Besides, you could have said *that* over the phone."

He finished the beer. "I know. But that's not what I want to talk about."

"As if I didn't know. And all the time I thought you wanted me to come down here just so you could say sweet things!"

He didn't feel much like banter. "I've been thinking about this morning."

Her smile fled and she was suddenly the university intellectual again. "Is there anything left to say? I'm about talked out."

He started ticking them off on his fingers. "One, why did our friend fill out the questionnaire accurately in the first place?"

"We discussed that this afternoon and decided that, inferior beings that we are, it would be impossible to guess his motives. Cat and mouse, maybe. I don't know."

"Two, is he some sort of mutation or just a human being operating at a hundred per cent efficiency?"

She cocked her head. "As one of your students might say, you're not getting through, Professor."

"I mean, a human being might be capable of more than we would think. Take Kuda Bux . . ."

"Kuda who?"

"B-u-x. He's a Hindu who was born in Kashmir about fifty-five years ago. Used to give demonstrations and for all I know, he still does. I once read a report in the *British Medical Journal* of a demonstration where he walked on fire. The temperature was eight-hundred degrees Fahrenheit and Bux was in the heat for four and a half seconds. He got through it all right but when a medical student tried to duplicate it, his feet were blistered so badly they bled."

Marge started to interrupt and Tanner put a finger on her lips. "That's not all. He used to ride a motorcycle around town when he was blindfolded. He could also read books that way. And he could read them by holding his hand in front of the printed page; apparently he had trained some of the cells of his skin to act as sight receptors. Maybe it's not impossible—the eyes and the skin both develop from the same embryonic ectoderm."

"Were these authenticated?"

"Yes."

She shivered. "I don't know if I like that any better than your mutation."

Tanner looked down at the table and ran his fingers through the damp ring the beer mug had left. "Third, and most important, what do you think our friend's attitude will be towards the human race? That may be more important than our attitude towards him, you know."

"I don't know. I suspect the all-father attitude. He probably feels all the love, care and affection towards human beings that we feel towards dogs."

"Meaning that those of us who have the same adoring attitude towards him that our pets have for us are the ones who will get along?"

"That's right. And I'm ready to build a little shrine in my living room just as soon as I know what to put in it. And what kind of incense to burn." She finished her drink, the first time that Tanner could remember seeing her gulp one. "Maybe we're doing him an injustice—we don't even know what he wants." She toyed with her glass. "What do you think about it?"

"I'm not quite sure. I think I feel more like I did when I was a kid and played Power for the first time."

"Power?"

"It's a kid's game. A player and his confederate leave the room for a moment and the group that stays behind picks out an object. When they come back, the confederate is let in on it and asks his partner, 'Is it the piano? Is it the lamp?' and so on. He doesn't look at his partner and his voice doesn't vary but when he mentions the object the group has chosen, his partner says, 'Yes, it's the sofa'—or whatever it happens to be. If any other player can guess how they did it, he says, 'I've got the Power!' "

"What's the trick?"

"It's simple, actually. Just before the real thing, the confederate asks his partner if it's any object that happens to be colored black. This is the tip-off that the next item he calls is it. But until you catch on to it, they've really got you going." He hesitated. "You get to believing that it's true, that the kid can really read minds. You resent it and you're envious as all hell that somebody has the Power and you don't. I felt a little that way this morning, along with being frightened as all get-out."

He paused. "This evening I started to think what a terrific piece of scientific research he would be."

Marge's voice turned sarcastic. "I know how you could finance it. Maybe you could get our friend to give testimonials. You know: 'The Better Man eats Oat Flakes,' or, 'The Man of

Tomorrow drives a Super-Six Sedan.' Do you have any idea how you could make him hold still for your research?"

He went back to finger painting on the damp table. "You consider him a menace, don't you?"

"Don't you?"

"Not necessarily. Why should he be? What would he want?"

"The usual things. Power, money, love."

He shook his head. "Those are human desires. They wouldn't necessarily apply to him, you know."

"They wouldn't necessarily *not* apply, either. You're looking at him as being superior in every department. I think you're mistaken. I think he's limited."

"Why?"

She shrugged. "Maybe I'm reading too much into it. But why did he show himself at all? John dared him, and he responded. That's a very human thing to do—to give in to a dare."

He thought about it for a moment. "You think he might be sort of a Johnny one-note, then? A one-fault Jones? A few superior talents and . . ."

". . . and very human failings. And I think the combination is dangerous, like a three-hundred-horsepower motor in a nineteen-fifteen car body."

"Just what do you think his talents might be?"

"I really don't have any idea. And I hope I never find out."

There was a little silence between them and for the first time he became aware of the slight hum of conversation in the room. Finally he said, "I'll give him the benefit of a doubt, Marge. I think he might be all right. It's a human reaction to be afraid of something we don't understand and I think that half the time we cut our own throats when we are. I know one thing: I'd like to find out who it is."

She lowered her voice. "Bill, what about the government? Don't you think you ought to notify them?"

"Maybe they'd think we were all a little off."

"That's not a good reason."

"I know. So I tried to place a call from the laboratories."

"And?"

"The phone wasn't working." She looked startled and he said dryly, "Don't let your imagination run away with you. A falling tree limb snapped the wires right at the insulators."

"You're sure of that?" She glanced at the other couples huddled over the polished wooden tables. "Lord, I'll never forget the look on Professor Scott's face!"

"Which one do you think it is?" Tanner asked abruptly.

"I'd almost rather not know."

"Nordlund?"

"I doubt it. He doesn't get along very well with people, which I think would be vitally necessary."

"It could be a pose."

"Maybe."

He hunched over the table. "What about Van Zandt?"

"That one I might buy." She frowned. "He's brilliant, he's cold, and he doesn't hide the fact that he holds the human race in low esteem."

"What do you know about him?"

"Not a great deal. Unhappy marriage, which is nothing unusual, I guess. He and Susan met during the war. He was a captain in psychological warfare and she was a singer in one of the Chicago night clubs. He wanted to marry glamour and she wanted to marry a homebody. They were both disappointed."

"Grossman?"

"Physicist type. Believes strictly in what he can measure and doesn't believe in what he can't. At least, he didn't until this morning—and he was mumbling something about short-wave radiation when we left. By tomorrow he'll be denying that he saw it at all. He's supposed to be a genius, one who's on remarkably good terms with the common herd." She paused. "There're rumors that he uses a Linguaphone so he can keep his accent."

"No doubt a superior trait."

The waitress came back with more drinks and Tanner

buried himself in the beer for a moment. *Grossman is a possibility*, he thought. *There's no doubt that he's a superior human being. But just how superior?*

"What about Eddy DeFalco, Bill? You know him better than I do."

"His reputation is not exaggerated, if that's what you mean."

"I know all about Rosemary O'Connor—but that isn't what I meant."

He shrugged. "Sorry. Eddy's an odd combination. Animalistic, idealistic, and brainy. No conscience. He knows what he wants and goes all out to get it and to hell with society."

"He'd fit."

"Maybe."

"I suppose we can leave out Professor Scott."

"Why? There's nothing that says our superman has to be young, is there?"

She looked dubious. "No, I suppose not. It just doesn't seem logical, though."

"Things haven't seemed logical since nine o'clock this morning. What about John Olson himself?"

"The personality zero?"

He felt irritated. "So some time ago somebody stepped on him. It happens to a lot of people."

"It could be a cover-up."

If it was, it was one of the best, he thought. Olson was a nervous, finger-plucking, pale young man who made a fetish out of being cautious. He was the kind of man who wouldn't be positive about the time of day. Likable in a way—you felt sorry for him—but there was something unpleasant hidden behind the perpetually frightened eyes. Something so unpleasant you had the feeling that no matter what you guessed it to be, it was bound to be something worse.

"I would tend to eliminate John first of all," Marge said thoughtfully. "Which is probably the most logical reason for considering him."

"Then that leaves you and Petey."

"*Me!*"

He half smiled. "Why not? Superman doesn't have to be a *man*, you know."

"And it wouldn't do much good for me to deny it, would it?"

"That's just what you would be expected to do, under the circumstances."

"All right," she said coolly. "Then I don't deny it."

For a moment he felt like somebody had dropped an ice cube down his back. "How do I know you're kidding?"

"You don't," she said maliciously.

He drained the rest of his beer. "Let's talk about something else."

An hour later the bartender flicked the lights twice in rapid succession and Tanner glanced at his watch. Closing time—and early Sunday morning. He helped Marge on with her jacket and they stepped out into the night. Outside, a light fog had rolled in from the lake and it had started to mist. The dark clouds had settled so low that Tanner felt a slight touch of claustrophobia.

They started walking down the street and he brushed her hand with his. Their fingers met and clung.

"Do you ever get lonely, Marge?" He let it hang there.

"Sometimes."

"You don't have to be."

He could sense her smiling faintly in the dark. "Is this a proposal or a proposition?"

"You want an honest answer?"

"Naturally."

He was quiet for a moment. "All right, I'll be honest and call it both."

"You're nice, Bill."

"But not that nice?"

She seemed distant. "It's a cold night, isn't it?"

He walked her to her apartment, kissed her lightly on the cheek, and left her fumbling for the door key. He was at the bottom of the steps when she said, "Bill? John Olson called me earlier this evening and said you should be sure to look him up tomorrow. He said he had been trying to get hold of you all afternoon, he had something to tell you."

He wished to hell she had told him sooner. "I'll give him a ring in the morning."

She worked the key, then paused in the open doorway. "Bill?"

He whirled. "What?"

She was smiling down at him, half hidden in the darkness. "Good night."

He stared at the closing door, then turned and started down the street. It was only a mile back to his own apartment and there was no sense in waiting for a bus that might never come.

Street lamps on the shadowed streets, a haloed nimbus surrounding the globes. The store fronts dark and haunted, the pavement deserted. Life had retreated from the streets into snug little homes and apartments and rose-wallpapered bedrooms. It gave him the willies. It was as if the city were totally empty, mile after mile of desolate streets, a no-man's land with himself as the only living person. . . .

The click of his heels echoed back and forth from store to store—the solid, steady sound of leather hitting concrete. The solitary *click-click-click*, like the ticking of some huge watch.

He had covered three blocks before he caught the tiny separation in the sounds, the minute distinctions between the sound of his own heels on the sidewalk and the sound of someone else's a block down. So he wasn't the only one out late at night, he thought. In a way, it spoiled the illusion. . . .

He turned a corner and crossed over a block. The footsteps that paralleled his own also turned a corner and crossed over a block.

He changed step, just to vary the rhythm.

A block away, somebody else changed step.

Sweat oozed out on his forehead and the pounding of his

heart filled his ears. He stopped under an awning to light a cigarette and the flame jiggled uncertainly in his hands. His palms
felt damp and greasy.

If somebody was after him, he'd wait for them to come; he
could take care of himself. And if it was just somebody out walking, he'd wait for the sound to die away.

Thirty seconds.

One minute.

Five minutes.

There was no sound except the rising wind and the rustle of
leaves. He forced a smile. It had been his imagination. He'd
been acting like a kid sidling past a graveyard.

He started walking.

And there were the sounds of footsteps a block away. A little faster. He quickened his own step.

It hit him just when he was walking past a street lamp and
he had to hold on to the post for support. It felt like being
slugged and for a moment he almost blacked out. Something
tore and buffeted at his mind, forcing the essential bit of personality that was *him* to scuttle into the dim recesses. For a
brief moment he felt the helpless inferiority of a very small man
in a very large room, as if he were drunk and there were a small
kernel of sobriety in the back of his mind wondering why he
was saying and doing the things that he was.

It passed quickly and he straightened up, no longer afraid of
the evening and the footsteps.

Footsteps. Odd he should have thought of them. There
were no footsteps other than his own. He had been walking
down the street in the middle of a deserted city. Alone.

Alone.

His mind plucked curiously at the word and it struck him
how appropriate it was. He had been alone all of his life. Alone
in this damned vale of tears that people called life. Alone in the
rabbit warrens of the cities.

The unfriendly city. The houses, the apartment buildings,
the stores—all frowning at him, dark and unfriendly. Like the
world. The whole, entire world.

He turned another corner and walked slowly towards the park. It loomed ahead, a darkened stretch of trees and winding paths and small, crouching hills. The string of street lamps wound through the hills like a gigantic pearl necklace. To the right there was . . . the lake.

He was sweating. His hands were shaking and the salt perspiration crept down his forehead and beaded into the corners of his eyes. He had a headache, a whopping big headache, and somewhere lost inside him a voice was crying: *not the lake, not the lake, not the lake!*

People didn't care, he thought. People never gave a damn about each other. About him. Marge would smile and kid him to his face but she didn't really mean it. And it was that way with everybody he knew. Not a single friend among them, not a single person who cared . . .

What was it the man had said? The epitaph? *He lived, he suffered, he died.*

But there was always the lake. The beautiful lake. The cool, black, rolling lake with the long concrete piers that fingered out into the friendly water, into depths where the level was well above a man's head. Just a few steps down the sloping sands and onto the concrete . . .

Not the lake!

William Tanner was going to die, he thought, and felt something salt crawl down his cheek. Little Willie Tanner whose mother had died when he was eight, despite everything the Science practitioner could do. And whose father had been killed in an airplane accident, one of those fateful accidents that you have a premonition about. *"I shouldn't go, Willie. I don't feel right about it. . . ."*

And now Mom and Dad and Grandma Santucci would be waiting for him and he'd show the people who didn't care. . . .

Just a few more steps to the pier. The black water, quietly lapping against the concrete in small waves that were getting bigger as the wind rose. The black-green, friendly water. Waiting for him.

He turned for one last look, his cheeks streaked with tears.

A man was standing at the head of the pier. A tall man, with a slouch hat that was pulled down over his face, wearing a belted raincoat. The man was waiting for him to take that long, last dive and Willie didn't want to disappoint him, did he?

No, Tanner thought. He didn't want to disappoint his friend. The friend who would call the police so they could fish out his body when they found it lodged against the pier supports below.

He turned back to the water. So restful, so peaceful . . .

"Hey, Mac, don't do it! For God's sake, don't go off!"

There was a moment of confusion and silent regret and then something sank out of his mind like water draining from a basin. He felt weak and collapsed to his knees on the pier, almost falling over the side. Two men were racing towards him, down the strip of concrete. Soldiers, from a couple of cars parked on the slight cliff overlooking the lake. Their dates were standing on the shore, the wet wind plastering their dresses against them.

The man in the belted raincoat was gone.

"What the hell's wrong, fella? You weren't going to go off, were you?"

His teeth were chattering and they had to help him to his feet.

"Tell us where you live, buddy, and we'll take you home. Life can't be that bad. A good night's sleep . . ."

"Not home," he mumbled. "Some all-night restaurant where they've got a big crowd . . . don't want to be alone."

They helped him back towards the shore. He was so damned weak, he thought. So damned out of it. And so miserably frightened.

Something had toyed with him, like a very superior cat toying with a very stupid mouse. He had been handled like a two-year-old. Somebody had pulled the strings and he had jerked like a marionette, doing what they wanted him to, thinking what they wanted him to think.

He was a strong man, physically and mentally, but he had

been handled like putty. A moment more and he'd have committed suicide. A dive into the lake and that would have been it.

Exit Professor Tanner. Exit the curious Professor Tanner who was in charge of a research project for the Navy and who had uncovered something that he shouldn't have. Exit Professor Tanner who was in a position to learn too much.

It started to rain harder, the water coming down in huge drops that splashed on the pier and made small explosions in the lake and wet his hair until it was plastered over his forehead like tape.

The soldiers had thrown his friend off, he thought. They could probably have been handled but they were unexpected and apparently it took time to gain control of a man's mind. So he had been saved. But at least it settled the questions that Marge had brought up earlier in the evening. Their friend was a menace and apparently his talents were limited. He had only one. One simple, terrible gift.

He could make people do what he wanted them to.

Tanner shivered and felt horribly sick. The night still reeked with murder and somewhere in the city a monster was loose.

3

THE soldiers took him to an all-night restaurant, had a cup of coffee with him, and left. After they had gone, he retrieved the Sunday papers that somebody had left behind and read everything including the want ads. Then he ordered more coffee and battled grimly with his nerves, looking up apprehensively every time somebody came in. When the morning finally came, he went to a Catholic church and sat through every Mass, hearing nothing of what was said but absorbing the comforting presence of the people in the pews. After lunch he went to a movie and saw a complete show. Twice.

People gave him a feeling of security, he was afraid to be without them. And he dreaded the evening when the streets would be empty and he would have to go home alone. He could go to the movies again, he thought—maybe take in an all-night feature. But the crowd would thin out at midnight and the interior of a deserted movie house would be just as bad as the lonely streets.

He finally went back up north to a druggist he knew and talked the man out of a small box of sleeping pills. Perhaps the danger was not in going to sleep but in staying awake. . . .

He roamed the crowded streets until six and then, without giving it any conscious thought, walked over to a little spaghetti house that was open Sunday night and which the bachelor faculty members had made their own particular hangout. He still hadn't called Olson. He hadn't gotten his courage up to that point.

He didn't frighten easy, he thought, but this time he was scared to the point where he was close to being physically sick. No longer to be his own master, to feel that he was being *used*, that somebody had—in effect—put him on as casually as they would put on a glove. . . .

He spotted Eddy DeFalco alone in one of the booths and immediately tried to shrink back out of sight. DeFalco was too good a bet, too logical a choice for whatever had stalked him the night before.

"Hey, Bill, let's be sociable—come on over!"

The restaurant was fairly crowded and he had a feeling that safety lay in numbers. He walked over woodenly and sat down.

DeFalco started to butter a thick slice of Italian bread. "You changing your diet? You've never had spaghetti on Sunday night before."

I'm not good at acting, Tanner thought. *I wonder if my suspicion shows. Have to be casual.*

"I'm not having it now, either. Just coffee."

DeFalco's eyes narrowed. "You look white as a sheet, Bill. Feeling okay?"

No, I don't Eddy. And maybe you know why. . . . "I guess I'm a little jumpy."

DeFalco looked sympathetic. "Everybody's upset. Nobody knows for sure yet whether it's coincidence or exactly what it is."

He had a curious feeling of disorientation, as if he and De-Falco were talking about two different things. "I wish to God that I had never gone to that meeting yesterday," he said carefully.

"Who doesn't? I'm not too happy I was there myself."

He couldn't help talking about it, even to DeFalco who might know all the answers. It was like reminding himself over and over that he wasn't going to use a certain word and then having the pressure build up until he had to. And Eddy might say something about it that would give him a clue. . . .

"Ed, how do you feel towards him?"

"What do you mean?"

"Do you dislike him, do you hate him?"

"You know damned well I'll feel towards him exactly the way he wants me to." DeFalco carefully wound up a forkful of spaghetti. "If I have my own way, I suppose I'll dislike him. In fact, I might even hate his guts."

"Why?"

"How well do you know me?"

Edward Marconi DeFalco, Tanner thought. Thick, black hair, high cheekbones, and full, sensuous lips. A beach-boy tan and physical build, just beginning to flesh out the way most athletes did later in life. The crooner type in light gray slacks and charcoal sport coat. A lot of men disliked him on sight and so did those women who considered him too "pretty" to be entirely masculine and then made the mistake of giving him a chance to prove it wasn't so.

"Nobody ever really knows anybody else, Ed."

"Then I'll tell you something. Everything I am, I've had to work for."

"Everybody . . ."

DeFalco held up his hand. "I don't mean it that way. By what I am, I mean personality and I know how tough it is even to define the word. A person's mannerisms, the way he acts, the little expressions he gets on his face—the things that go to make up the *you* that people remember. Like two kids selling popcorn in a ball park. One will make a mint and the other won't be able to move half a dozen bags. What's the difference? The personality."

He pushed the plate of spaghetti away and dabbed at his face with a napkin. "I manufactured my own personality. I mean it. I made a study of what people liked in other people and tried to develop those traits myself. Hell, I even used to stand in front of a mirror and practice my winning ways. And if that makes me a hypocrite without a sincere bone in my body, I'll admit it. But I only did consciously what every kid does unconsciously.

"And then I met a man who *was* a personality. He was the most alive person I ever met—there was more life in his little finger than in my whole body." He hesitated. "Don't get the wrong idea. I was running after little girls when I was nine years old. But like I say, I used to pal around with this friend of mine and you know what happened one day? I wasn't Eddy DeFalco any more. I was this other person down to the last little mannerism, down to the way he used to accent his words. His personality had run right over mine and I was a carbon copy clear down to my toenails."

He studiously stirred some sugar into his coffee. His voice was low. "As soon as I realized it, I hated him. But you see the same thing every day. Movie stars, athletes. People worship them, people copy them. People *want* to be an extension of somebody else's personality. Now just imagine what the world would be like with your superman running around."

Tanner sat there and felt the fear damming up within himself again. To a lesser extent it was exactly how he had felt on the pier. Run over, flattened, an extension of somebody else's personality. DeFalco had done an excellent job of describing it.

DeFalco drained his coffee and made a face. "People would only come in one model then. God knows I don't think too much of the human race sometimes but I would be willing to kill a man to avoid that."

Tanner studied him carefully. "Would you be willing to kill him if I told you who it was?"

DeFalco stared at him and Tanner felt his teeth want to chatter; he gripped the table to keep his hands from shaking. The intense dark eyes and the sullen, brooding face.

And behind it . . . ?

"You know, I suppose."

"I think John Olson knows. I think that's why Olson was scared to death yesterday morning."

DeFalco's face showed nothing. "So all we have to do is ask John, is that what you're driving at?"

"That's right. That's all we have to do."

"You haven't run into Marge or Petey or Karl or any of the others today, have you?"

"I haven't been around."

"Well, you won't be able to ask John Olson about it. Not tonight or tomorrow or any time."

He suspected what was coming. "Why not?"

DeFalco's voice was flat.

"Because John died at three o'clock this morning."

4

HE checked in at the neighborhood YMCA early Sunday night, when there were still people on the streets.

The night clerk was a little too prim and uncooperative. "I don't know, sir. We don't ordinarily rent rooms to people without baggage."

"It's only for one night. I . . . haven't any other place to stay."

The clerk's eyebrows arched slightly and Tanner guessed what the man was thinking. He could try to bribe him, he thought, but it would be expensive and the clerk impressed him as the type who would scream for the police.

"My wife," he said, looking sheepish. "We had an argument and you know how it is. Locked out and I don't want to call the cops and let the whole neighborhood know. By morning it'll probably blow over but right now . . ."

The clerk studied him a moment longer, then relented. He passed over a card for Tanner to sign and took a key off the rack behind him.

"It's on the sixth floor. Bathroom down the hall and there's a telephone by the stairway."

He took the elevator up and padded down the deserted hallway to his room. He went in, locked the door and jammed a chair in front of it. Then he switched off the light and stood to one side of the window, staring down at the street below. A few couples drifting by on the sidewalk, two or three customers in the delicatessen on the corner. But nobody in the shadows across the street, watching. Nobody in a parked automobile looking up at his window.

He opened the box of sleeping tablets and juggled one in his hand, debating whether or not he should take it. He was dead tired but he had so much on his mind that he wouldn't be able to sleep without it. Then it occurred to him that once asleep he might be easy prey for the questing mind that had almost driven him off the pier.

But nobody knew he was staying at the Y, did they?

It's a gamble, he thought. They could check his apartment and once they discovered he wasn't there, it wouldn't take too much trouble to track him down. But on the other hand he had already been one whole night without sleep and he was riding the rim of nervous exhaustion. He couldn't last it out another evening.

He took the pill.

When he awoke in the morning it was with a splitting headache and a confused recollection of a nightmare about the lake.

But the important thing was he was still alive.

He was jittery, he didn't want to go back to the campus. But there were classes to be taught and a salary to earn and in broad daylight his courage was several notches higher. And he didn't want to give in to the fear that he felt.

There were the same gray, gothic buildings and the same tired ivy crawling up them but somehow the campus was different. It wasn't hard to put his finger on it. The difference was in the students. Little knots of quietly gossiping collegians fell silent and stared at him with a bright-eyed curiosity as he walked past. A few feet away the whispers started up again and he knew they were rehashing every time he had said something to or about John Olson.

Whether he liked it or not, he was going to wear Olson around his neck like an albatross. Olson had been on his committee and Olson had been about the same age, so it would naturally be assumed that he had known Olson fairly well.

And that was one of the rubs. He had known Olson hardly at all.

Petey was sitting at her desk in his shoe-box office on the third floor, staring stonily out the window. Her hands were folded in her lap and her face looked as if it had been hewn from granite. Her hair had been pulled back into an even tighter bun than usual and she was wearing a black dress with a high, starched collar and long sleeves. The only touch of color was in the two pink, plastic combs in her hair, and that just made the rest of her seem more forbidding.

Petey in mourning, Tanner thought, looking ten years older than she actually was.

"You didn't have to come down, Petey."

"What else could I have done?" Her voice was mechanical and precise, without inflection. "There was nothing I could do at home or over at the Van Zandts'. The police told me that. So I came up here."

He wondered what she was actually seeing, staring out the window. Not the scenery, he was sure of that.

"I wish I could think of something clever and sympathetic, Petey. I guess all I can say is that I'm sorry."

"Everybody's sorry," she said slowly. "It's too bad that people don't feel sorrier for each other when they're alive."

Tanner felt uncomfortable. "I didn't know John very well."

"Nobody did."

"How did it happen? Do the police have any leads?"

She turned away from the window. "Leads?"

"Leads on who killed your brother," he said, watching her face carefully.

The look of granite crumbled at the edges. "Who said anything about John being killed?"

He felt like he was in one of those conversations where you talk with somebody for ten minutes and then discover that each of you is talking about something else. But it shouldn't have been like that this time, he thought. They should have been talking about the same thing.

About who had murdered John Olson.

"Tell me about it, Petey."

She wet her lips. "I don't know too much about it. Susan Van Zandt found him—the body—at seven in the morning. He had set the alarm so he could go to Mass and it went off and rang and kept on ringing. When nobody turned it off, Susan went up and knocked on the door. There wasn't any answer so she used her key and went on in."

While she was talking, Petey tightened her fingers around a crumpled wad of handkerchief, twisting the cloth until Tanner thought she would tear it. Her fingers looked thin and hard and scrawny.

"John had been sitting at his desk, writing a letter. He never finished it. He was slumped in his chair, half lying on the desk. Later on, the police said he had been dead for four hours, that he had died at three in the morning."

"Stop it, Petey. I'm sorry I asked you."

"The detective said there had been no struggle," she continued with a horrible, dry-eyed composure. "John hadn't been shot or knifed or blackjacked or strangled, he had just . . ."

"Petey, do you have any friends who might be home today?"

The starched face nodded silently.

"Then take the day off and go and see them. Come back whenever you feel up to it. Next week, maybe two weeks . . ."

After she had left, he went to the window and stared out, trying to regain his sense of proportion. There was the green grass three stories below, the ivy that trailed up the broken brick to frame his one window, and the small, industrious spider that had cast its web in the upper left-hand corner. Two flies buzzed futilely just outside the pane: the first signs of summer. In a nearby tree, a squirrel chittered angrily at him and on the lawn below, a student stretched out to doze and forget the worlds of Chaucer and Shakespeare.

There was nobody watching the building, nobody at all.

He brewed himself a cup of scorching hot, black coffee, then went to class and lectured to a suddenly wide-awake audience that was far more interested in the death of John Olson than in anthropology. He bluntly parried questions about it, dismissed the class, and went to lunch.

Early in the afternoon he dropped in on Susan Van Zandt.

The house that John Olson had died in was an old-fashioned, white clapboard affair that had been built around the turn of the century. It was a landmark the university had acquired in a will and promptly turned into a faculty home. It was set far back on a huge corner lot. Two oak trees stood sentry duty near the front walk while a small row of shrubs ringed the sides of the house. The shrubs were a tired, speckled green, dusted with small flakes of white paint that had chalked and run off the clapboards during the rainy season.

The interior of the house looked incomplete. A wall had been knocked out between the living and the dining rooms to make one room that was much too large for the furniture it contained. Worn oak flooring showed at the edges of a large, floral-patterned rug that hadn't been quite big enough. It barely crept under the edges of a sagging sofa by the window and lapped just over the edge of the brick apron of a fireplace that had been painted white in an attempt to make it look modernistic. A black-oak tea table sprawled in front of the sofa, half hidden beneath dog-eared magazines and a square, glass ash tray that had been emptied but not washed so a fine crust of gray ash still clung to the bottom.

A desk stood by the fourth wall, under guard of a straight-backed, wooden chair with a hand-hooked woolen seat cushion of roses against a background of blue. Next to the desk, along the wall, was a radiator with a tin cover, green paint peeling in spots. A small coffee tin of stagnant water stood on top of it.

A lived-in, rumpled room that somehow reminded Tanner of Susan Van Zandt herself.

She had let him in, smiled a dutiful smile, and relaxed gratefully back on the couch. She still had her bathrobe on and Tanner knew there would be dust on the mantel, dishes in the sink, and an icebox full of slowly souring leftovers. Her thick, brown hair wasn't brushed and her eyes had the faintest suggestion of circles beneath them. She had been slim and attractive at one time, he thought, but after marriage she had slipped easily into an early middle age and had let motherhood coarsen her. She hadn't regretted either one.

"I don't think John ever roomed anyplace else," she said nervously. "Central Housing sent him over here as soon as he showed up on campus. I think he always liked it here." She waved her hand around the room. "It's comfortable and then he had his own key and could come and go as he pleased."

"Did he ever go out much?" Tanner asked. "Did he ever have any friends that he went out drinking with, anything like that?"

"No, he never had many friends."

He lit his pipe and toyed with the match a moment before letting it fall into the tray. "The night he died. Had he had any visitors earlier that evening? Anybody who might have stayed behind for a good part of the night?"

"No, I don't recall any. He went out for a walk and when he came in he told Harold and myself that he was tired, that he was going to do some reading and write a letter or two."

"Sue." He hesitated a moment, wondering how he should phrase it. "Do you know if anybody on campus hated him enough to kill him?"

The heavy-lidded eyes flew open. "Oh, no. He wasn't killed.

The police said there were no signs of a struggle or a fight. He had been writing a letter when it . . . happened."

"Can I see the room?"

She pulled her faded bathrobe tighter around her stomach and led the way to the second floor. Olson's room was a door down from the bathroom. She worked a key in the lock. "I don't know why I keep it locked up like this but the police asked me not to touch anything and I guess this is the best way." She was suddenly doubtful. "Maybe I shouldn't let you in."

"Don't worry, Sue, I won't disturb anything."

She opened the door and he walked in. The windows were closed and the room smelled a little musty. Sunlight slanted through faded curtains, highlighting a miniature of the downstairs rug and a small, blue throw rug by the side of the bed. The bed was neatly made, the pink, tufted chenille spread smooth and unwrinkled.

"Did you make up the bed?"

"No, I guess he just didn't sleep in it."

"About what time did he get in?"

"About an hour after you called. Midnight, I guess. Van and I were watching TV."

John Olson had come in at midnight and died at three, Tanner reasoned. For three hours he had sat in his room—doing what? And then he had put on his bathrobe and sat down to write a letter. To whom? And what about?

One thing was almost certain, however. He could eliminate Van. It was hardly likely that Olson would be living in the same house if Van . . .

Or was it? Van Zandt had been watching Olson like an eagle in the seminar room. Waiting for Olson to say something? To give him away?

He glanced at his watch and breathed a little easier. Van Zandt had classes all afternoon; he wouldn't be around.

"Is the letter still here, Sue?"

"No, the police lieutenant has it. I . . . never got a look at it."

He glanced around the room again. A small, oak bureau

with a dust-soiled dresser scarf on it. A desk by one side of the window, a half-open closet door showing a few hangers with a drab gray suit, a gray topcoat, and a rack of small-figured, dull ties.

There was a blue blanket tacked on the wall over the desk. In the middle of it was a large gold felt "B," with "Basketball" embroidered on it in small blue script.

It didn't fit.

"I never knew John went in for sports. He never seemed like the type."

"I don't think he was, either. He never talked about them and never seemed to have any interest in them."

"But he still won a letter in basketball."

She was standing by the window looking out into the back yard. She was watching her two boys play in the yard, he guessed. Already John Olson was fading when compared to the really important things in her life.

"It doesn't add up, does it?" she said absently.

Tanner walked over to the desk. It was a plain desk, varnished a dark, almost black, color. A photograph on top caught his eye. It was a picture of Olson and Petey at a faculty picnic earlier in the spring. Petey was, as usual, a little too carefully dressed for a picnic. But at least she was smiling at the camera and with what seemed like a genuine smile.

Her brother wasn't smiling. But then John Olson never had, as long as he could remember. A plump, serious face with strands of blond hair hanging limply over his high forehead. A suggestion of a slouch in his shoulders and he could even tell from the photo that Olson was pale and soft under his sport shirt. He guessed that John had been worried about getting sunburned and was getting ready to give Petey hell for having dragged him out there.

"Do you know much about him, Sue? Much about his background?"

She tore herself away from the window and walked over to the chair to sit down, the robe swaying against her flanks and her slippers making small slapping sounds against the rug.

"Give me a cigarette, Bill." He gave her one and lighted it. "He came from a small town in South Dakota. Brockton, I think. His people were farmers. He lived there until he was eighteen when he went away to college."

"That doesn't tell me much about him."

She spread her hands. "That's all I know. He never talked much about himself."

"He had a pretty cold personality. Any reason why?"

She closed her eyes and frowned, as if trying to remember were hard work and she wasn't quite up to it. "Who knows? I think maybe somebody hurt him when he was young. I always got the impression that the only real emotion he felt for anybody was hatred for somebody back in his home town."

"Did he ever talk much about it?"

"I told you he never talked about himself at all."

"Anything else?"

"Nothing moved him very much," she said finally. "Other people's problems didn't interest him at all, probably because he was so wrapped up in his own. He was . . . cold . . . and he had no sense of humor. And I think he was frightened of something."

"Any idea what of?"

"No, except it was some person. Maybe the same person in his home town that he hated. And I could be wrong on that score, too."

He looked around the room again. Dusty little room. The bed, the bureau, and the bookcase, shelves jammed with textbooks. If you went away for a day and let the dust settle you wouldn't think anybody had lived in it for years.

"Was he pretty much the intellectual?"

"Yes and no. He was interested in psychology, but then that was his field. I would say he was more interested in the offbeat side, though. Hypnotism, things like that." She walked over to the window again and ran her fingers slowly down the curtains. "I'm sorry that he's dead."

It was the thing to say, Tanner realized. But he hoped when he died and somebody said it, that they would say it with more emotion.

The doorbell rang downstairs and Susan turned away from the window and started for the stairs.

"The detective—he was supposed to come back today."

Lieutenant Crawford was middle-aged, with pale-blue eyes and a friendly face and hair that was beginning to silver around the temples and above the ears. He wore a slouch hat and a blue suit with a suggestion of a shine and a lived-in air and signs of strain where it was tight around the waist. He looked a lot like a harried, unsuccessful businessman.

Tanner introduced himself and Crawford grunted, found a place for his hat on the bureau, and lowered himself into the straight-backed chair by the desk like a man lowering himself into a tub of steaming hot water.

"Mrs. Van Zandt told me about you downstairs, Tanner. Nice woman isn't she?"

"Real nice," Tanner said shortly.

"Not a very good housekeeper but I guess she doesn't have the background for it." He teetered the chair back on its two rear legs and stared at the room, then looked back at Tanner. "You knew John Olson pretty well, didn't you?"

"Not too well. His sister is my secretary. And John was on my committee. Outside of that, I didn't know him very well at all."

"Meaning you probably didn't like him too well. I guess nobody else did, either."

"I didn't say that, Lieutenant."

"You didn't have to. You talk to as many people as I have and you get so you can tell attitudes. Olson was a nobody. Nobody liked him very well, nobody thought very much of him, and nobody's too sad now that he's dead." He took a cigar from his coat pocket and neatly circumcised the end with a penknife. "We get them every day. Usually down in the city and usually in a rented sleeping room. The relatives live way off to hell and gone, they've got no friends, and the county has to foot the funeral bill." He sounded bitter. "You'd be surprised how little people care about each other, Professor."

He leaned forward in his chair. "Now this committee he was on. What was it all about?"

"Research for the Navy—confidential work but I can tell you a little about it. We were testing human beings to see how they would stand up under battle conditions. What the breaking point is. That sort of thing."

Crawford chewed it over for a moment, then looked at him shrewdly. "You want to know how he died, don't you? That why you waited?"

Tanner tried to keep the tenseness out of his voice. "That's right. I want to know how he died."

"His sister probably told you all we know. No external wounds, no shots or stabs. No blood at all. No signs of a struggle, no marks on the throat, no needle punctures on the arms. The missus says he didn't have any visitors and the windows weren't forced at any time."

"Have you got any theories?"

"Theories? That's the nice thing about my work, the woods are always full of them. Myself, I think he took the short way out. We won't know until we get the results of the autopsy but it looks like poison." He took the cigar out of his mouth and stared at the chewed end thoughtfully. "Did you ever see the expression on the face of a man who took poison? You wouldn't forget it, once you did. They die relatively slowly and feel every second of it. It all shows in the face." He shrugged. "The only thing wrong with that theory is that we can't find the bottle or the tin or whatever he carried it in."

"I don't think he would have taken poison," Tanner said.

"Why not? He wasn't well liked, he didn't have any friends or love life, and so far as I can tell, he didn't particularly enjoy living. We run into this type of thing all the time." He squinted at Tanner. "You must have your own ideas—people usually do."

"I think he was murdered," Tanner said slowly.

Crawford looked interested. "What's the motive? Money? Passion? Revenge? People usually have to have a reason for killing somebody."

There were plenty of reasons, Tanner thought. *Shall I tell you what it's all about, Lieutenant?*

"I still think he was murdered."

"You're entitled to your opinion, Professor. But I wouldn't want to be too sure of it. The only person who could be sure that Olson was murdered at this stage of the game would be the murderer himself."

"Anybody could think it was murder, Lieutenant. That's the popular thing to think nowadays."

"Yeah, I guess it is at that." Crawford took out his wallet and thumbed methodically through the bills and the cards. He moistened a thumb and pulled out a small, white card. "I found this taped down to the desk top and pulled it off and took it along. I didn't know what to make of it."

He handed the card over. It was in Olson's handwriting and read:

"*Man is a rope stretched between the animal and the Superman—a rope over an abyss. What is great in man is that he is a bridge and not a goal. . . .*"

It was signed: *Adam Hart.*

Tanner read it and handed it back. "I don't understand. It's a quotation from Nietzsche."

Crawford smiled slightly. "That's what the girl at the library said. This Adam Hart—ever hear of him, Professor?"

"No, I never heard of him before in my life."

"That so." Crawford gazed thoughtfully out the window and Tanner realized with a shock that the man didn't believe him. "That kind of surprises me, Professor, it really does." He leafed through his wallet again. "You know, I was rather glad I met you here. I was going to have to look you up later in the day, anyway. On business. You see, Olson was writing a letter when he died—he died right in the middle of it." He paused. "It was addressed to you, Professor."

He handed over a sheet of folded, blue writing paper and

Tanner opened it. The bottom right-hand corner was crumpled, as if a hand had suddenly clutched at it. On the paper itself there was just the date and his name and one line of writing that broke off abruptly.

PROFESSOR TANNER:

I want to tell you about Adam Hart——

5

HE went home late that afternoon and discovered his apartment had been thoroughly ransacked. The janitor remembered nothing, though nobody could have gotten in without his help. And he hadn't been bribed to forget, Tanner thought. The man honestly couldn't remember.

The next three nights were bad. He stored most of his possessions and lived out of a suitcase, shifting hotels every night and telling nobody where he was staying. There was nobody he could trust.

He locked the doors and stuffed clay into the keyholes and jammed the spring locks so they couldn't be forced open. Then he pulled the shades and sat in the dark and watched the streets or the courtyards through the crack between shade and window, waiting for the

Enemy to show up. He cradled his service pistol in his lap, hoping for the opportunity to use it.

David and Goliath, he thought grimly, *but I don't have a chance.* He would watch for an hour, then take a sleeping pill and collapse on the bed, not even bothering to turn down the sheet. Before he drifted off to sleep he usually spent an agonizing few minutes wondering what the Enemy's next move would be. He didn't have long to wait.

His world started to go smash Thursday morning.

He had been sitting at his desk going over his lectures for the day when Lieutenant Crawford walked in and settled in Petey's swivel chair. He looked worn; his shirt stuck to him in huge patches where the sweat had soaked through and little tears of perspiration oozed over the ridges in his neck.

"You could have knocked."

"Sorry, Professor—the door was open." Crawford turned in the chair to look out the window at the students crossing the quadrangle below. "Semester's just about over, isn't it?"

"Next week is finals. After that they're on their own."

"I've got a boy," Crawford mused. "He'll be coming home then. Leech off the old man or be a beach boy for the summer. Kids nowadays—they don't like to work any more. I guess we bring them up all wrong, we give them too much." He mopped at his face with a khaki handkerchief that was too small for the job. "What are you going to do this summer, Professor?"

Crawford had something to say but he was going to take his own sweet time in saying it, Tanner thought.

"I was thinking of taking a short leave from the Project and going out to Colorado on a research grant. Excavation of an old Indian village." With everything that had happened in the last few days, he knew he wasn't going to go. But Crawford would find that out in due time.

"You know, I rather figured that you would be doing something like that. I really did. But I guess we were both wrong."

Tanner studied Crawford for a moment. The man was a little too casual, he was waiting for some kind of reaction. "I don't get you."

"Being curious is my job so I checked up on it. No particular reason and if you want to get sore about my snooping, I guess you've got a right to be. Anyway, I checked and they told me in the front office that they had taken your name off the list. Just the other day, too. They're bringing in a professor from another university to handle it. They'd been considering him and at the last minute I guess he got it." He located a toothpick in his pocket and absently dug at a rear tooth. "I'm surprised you didn't know about it."

"I've got a contract," Tanner said tightly.

Crawford looked sympathetic. "I know people who have had contracts before, Professor. And guess what? They were no good—no good at all. I suppose you could sue but I wouldn't want to give you odds on winning."

"You're sure of this?"

"I don't kid people about things like this, Professor."

He had been going to withdraw anyway, Tanner thought. But he couldn't understand why his name should have been taken off the list arbitrarily.

"About John Olson," Crawford said, changing the subject. "The other day when I was talking to you, you said you thought he'd been murdered. Anything to go on besides your own opinion? This is official—and I wouldn't advise withholding information."

Tanner chose his words carefully. "Let's just say it was a hare-brained idea of mine. There was nothing solid to it."

"Then you weren't convinced to the point where you'd try playing detective?"

"What do you mean?"

"I'll put it this way. Sometimes a fellow dies and his friends or relatives think he was done in. And when it turns out that he wasn't and the police close the case, they get upset and start doing some investigation of their own. Usually they don't accomplish much but they make a lot of trouble for themselves and for the police. You understand?"

"I'm not sure."

Crawford looked pained. "I think maybe they read too many books. The ones in which the police are always stupid and overlook clues that any half-wit can find. Or maybe the police just don't want to solve it. Things aren't like that in real life, Professor. Ninety per cent of the time, when the police close the case it's because there's nothing more that can be done, or needs to be done."

Tanner felt tired. "Let's not beat around the bush, Lieutenant. What're you driving at?"

Crawford patted his face with his handkerchief again. "There's nothing more that needs to be done with the Olson case. We're closing it."

"I thought you had the idea that he was poisoned."

"So I was wrong. The results of the autopsy came in yesterday. There wasn't any poison, Professor. Not a trace of it." He smoothed out the dampened handkerchief and tucked it carefully away in a pocket. "I'll admit that the look on his face was almost a sure tip-off for poison, though it doesn't explain why he should've sat down to write you a letter rather than one to his sister, for example."

"Or who Adam Hart is."

Crawford snipped the end of a fresh cigar. "Adam Hart. I'll admit I'm curious about him, Professor. But then I'm curious about a lot of things and life's too short to investigate them all." He changed the subject. "Olson himself. Was he fairly healthy? Or was there something wrong that you know about? Something that might not show up in a routine physical?"

"So far as I know he was healthy. He never missed a class and he never seemed to suffer from chronic headaches or colds. Why?"

Crawford stood up, toying with his hat. "Well, I guess that's the way it goes then. I've seen it happen before to a young fellow so I shouldn't be too surprised."

Tanner could feel his skin start to crawl. "Surprised at what?"

"Olson wasn't killed and he didn't commit suicide, Professor. I hate to disappoint you but he came home at midnight Saturday night, read a while, and at three o'clock Sunday morning he sat down at his desk and died." He snapped his fingers. "Just like that. No pain or strain. He just died."

Just like that, he thought, after Crawford had gone. A young, relatively healthy man had sat down at his desk and died. With no cause.

He shivered. It would be so damned easy to get the shakes and end up in a blue funk, just knowing what was after him. Not *who*. Not a person, not somebody he could fight, not somebody he could flush out into the open.

Not *who*, but *what*.

And just what was wanted of him? To drop off the committee? Or had he already gone past the point of no return, did he already know too much? And if so, why hadn't there been another attempt to kill him? It wouldn't be difficult. Sunday morning he had almost walked off the end of the pier. Perhaps some day he would step out in front of an automobile or lean too far out of an open window. And everybody would say that Professor Tanner had been careless. Or that the world had been too much for him.

And why me? Why me rather than anybody else on the committee? What do I know that's so special? Or is it that he just hasn't gotten around to the others yet?

He started sifting through the pile of mail on his desk. It was the same stack of mail that had been there Wednesday morning. The same stack that had been there Tuesday and Monday. Nobody had sent him anything since Monday. No firm in the city had dropped him a circular, nobody had sent any bills.

He flicked through the sheaf of letters waiting to be filed and stopped at one. A colored circular from Colorado advertising the natural wonders of that state.

Only he wasn't going there. And one of the minor reasons why was that Crawford had said the school had dropped him. Why, he didn't know. Professor Scott wouldn't have had anything to do with it. He had had run-ins with Scott, but the old man had always backed him up outside of the department. His trouble must have started with the dean of the school, Harry Connell.

He looked at his watch. Harry would be in now. And maybe Harry would have an explanation.

Connell's secretary didn't want to let him by.

"I'm sorry, Bill. Mr. Connell's very busy right now. Why don't you stop back later?"

"Do you think he would be in later?"

She bit her lip. "Honest, Bill, I don't know what to say. He said you might drop by to see him and to tell you that he was busy."

"And that he was going to be busy the rest of the week, that it?"

She shrugged. "Of course, if you didn't pay any attention to me and walked right in . . . I can always say I tried."

He brushed past her. "Thanks."

The man in the office was on the phone, talking. He hung up when Tanner barged in, an angry look on his fleshy face.

"I thought I told my secretary to tell you I was busy?"

"She did but I guess I'm getting a pretty thick skin." He lowered his voice. "What's going on, Harry? Why didn't you let me know if something was up?"

Connell's face reddened. "I ought to call the police. I ought to have you thrown out of here but I'm trying to keep it quiet. The publicity wouldn't do the school any good and I kept thinking that we could ease you out and still keep it under cover. We were going to tease you along to the end of the semester and then we were going to lower the boom. But you want it lowered now."

"What on God's green earth are you talking about?"

Connell stood up and leaned his knuckles on the desk. "We pulled you from the Colorado field trip, Tanner, because it's our policy not to send out research groups of students unless they're under competent instructors."

"And I'm not?"

"Where did you get your degree?"

"Wisconsin."

"Can you prove it?"

Tanner sank down in a chair, enormously tired. "What's the story, Harry?"

Connell's mouth was so tight with anger it was almost invisible. "The name is *Mr.* Connell, Tanner. And the reason why I don't call you 'Professor' is because you're not one." He ran a shaking hand through his thinning hair. "It was a routine check—I don't know what made me do it. You had applied for the Colorado position and we wrote to Wisconsin asking for any experience you might have had on field trips before." He paused. "They never even heard of you. They don't have a single record of you. I've read about impersonations before but I never thought . . ."

Tanner was desperate. "You couldn't have checked everything!"

"We even went through the annual. . . ."

"I never had my picture taken for it."

"That's a little unusual, isn't it? And you didn't go out for any school activities, either, did you? We checked all of them."

"I was never much of a rah-rah boy. But you could've checked with Professor Palmer in the Anthropology Department. He could have told you."

Connell picked up a letter from his desk top and waved it at him. "He told us he never heard of you. Read it yourself."

"My thesis is on file here," Tanner said slowly. "You must have checked that."

"We checked it—that is, we tried to. There wasn't a thing. Not a thing."

"I filed it when I applied here, it should have been there!"

"Then why don't you go and look? And when you find it, bring it back here and I'll apologize." He picked up a narrow slip of paper from his desk and handed it to Tanner. "Here's a check—you're paid up to date. We're breaking your contract right now. You're through, both here and on the Project. You're lucky the board doesn't prosecute but it would make the university look foolish for having hired you in the first place."

Tanner took the check and stared blankly as the little man

turkey-walked back to his desk. All his records had been checked at one time, he thought, confused. They never would have hired him without doing that. Connell must realize that. Or maybe it was just that . . . that . . .

That Connell didn't remember.

His thesis wasn't listed in the card catalogue and when he checked in the stacks, he couldn't find it there, either. There was the row of neatly typed and bound theses, thick with dust, but there was no gap where one had been taken out. So far as he could determine, it had never been on file.

He sat in the stacks for half an hour before he got to his feet and walked outside. There was nothing to do but make plans to leave, to close down his bank account and get out of town. What he would do after that he didn't know and didn't care. But maybe now the waiting and the suspense was over. The Enemy had won and he was off the committee and in disgrace. No job, no source of income, no money coming in.

Down, but not quite out. At least, he wouldn't starve.

The teller at the bank took his book and came back a moment later, looking puzzled.

"I'm sorry, Mr. Tanner, but there seems to be some sort of a mix-up. We have no records here of any account for you."

The sun was shining and there wasn't a cloud in the sky, Tanner thought, but it was still going to be a lousy day. "Where do you think I got the book? Who do you think made out the entries?"

The teller fluttered his hands helplessly. "There's no record sheet for you and no identification card that we ask all depositors to sign. I don't know how this all happened. Really, I . . ."

Tanner's voice was thick. "Why don't you get the manager?"

The manager was a thin, balding man with steel-framed glasses and darting, suspicious eyes. He glanced at the bank book, frowned, and went to a rack of cards at the rear of the teller's cage. When he came back he had another book like the one Tanner had been issued.

"This book you have—it's yours?"

"It's got my name on it."

The manager gave him a nasty look and showed him the book he held in his hand. "It so happens we already have a book by the same number. The man to whom it was issued has held it for the last ten years. I don't know how you got hold of this book and numbered it and I don't know how you got it filled out but forgery is a criminal offense."

He suddenly stopped and looked as if he wished he had called the police immediately.

Tanner left him standing there and walked out.

He had had close to a thousand dollars in the bank and now it was down the drain. Somebody had gotten there ahead of him. Somebody who had pulled his card and substituted another. Or, to be more exact, somebody had persuaded the teller to pull the card.

You can't run very far without money.

Then he remembered and felt in his coat pocket. The check. He had never gotten around to cashing it at the bank. But there were half a dozen currency exchanges he knew of offhand.

The first one he tried cashed it without question and he felt momentarily pleased at the small victory. Then he realized, at best, he had just postponed the situation.

He stopped in at a small restaurant and ordered coffee. He felt worn out, as if he had run a mile or had been sick for a long time. The noose was drawing tighter. Any day, any hour, somebody would yank on the rope and he'd be left dangling. The Enemy obviously wanted something more than just to get him off the committee.

Why him?

He looked at the restaurant clock. Twelve o'clock, and he had an appointment with the dentist for one.

He fumbled through his pockets for a dime. It had been only a cleaning job and that could be put off to another day. And probably another city, since he wasn't going to be in this one too much longer.

He dialed the number, gave his name to the receptionist, and asked for a cancellation. There was a moment of silence.

"Would you repeat your name, sir?"

He did.

"I'm sorry, sir, but we have no appointment for anybody named Tanner."

"I made it a week ago," he said slowly. "For one o'clock."

Another pause.

"Dr. Landgraf doesn't recall you, Mr. Tanner. However, if you wish to make an appointment . . ."

He hung up.

No mail since Monday. Because his name had somehow disappeared from all the lists? Because all the files that mentioned him had been yanked? And there was the case of the records in Wisconsin and the disappearance of his thesis from the library. And then the bank book and his appointment with the dentist . . .

He was being isolated, he thought. Anything in print that mentioned his name was disappearing. People were being conditioned to forget that he had ever existed. One by one his connections with people were being severed. It was like a dental surgeon blocking off the nerves with shots of Novocain.

Just before the tooth was pulled.

6

THEY buried John Olson Friday morning.

It was in a little cemetery just outside the city limits, on a morning that was overcast and cloudy with a
cold wind that blew off the choppy lake.

The priest stood at the head of the grave and said a
few words, words that were tumbled and lost in the
wind that flapped his vestments. Then the two
gravediggers worked the small rollers that held the canvas straps supporting the coffin and it lurched and
slowly disappeared into the raw gash of the earth.

Tanner watched it with a morbid fascination, then
glanced at the small crowd gathered on the other side
of the grave. There was Petey, in a long, black dress
and a heavy veil, leaning on Marge's arm. Karl Gross-

man, fat and thoughtful and neatly dressed for once. Harold Van Zandt and Susan and Eddy DeFalco. Professor Scott, wrapped in a muffler and a greatcoat and looking almost ready for the last rites himself. And Commander Nordlund, with an appropriately sorrowful expression on his face that was probably more because of a missed golf game than Olson's death. Harry Connell and a few other faculty members.

None of Olson's relatives, outside of Petey, were present.

The priest walked over and said something to Petey and they started for the line of cars on the road a few hundred feet away. The others followed, Tanner with them. Behind him he could hear the soft sound of shovels biting into the dirt.

There had been nine of them at the meeting on Saturday morning, he thought. And that had included one very frightened personality-cripple who had tried to convince the rest of them that the human race was living on borrowed time. Now there were only eight and that was counting another very frightened soul who was slated for elimination.

Himself.

The others hadn't had much to say to him but he detected an uneasiness about them, a suspicion of each other. They had seemed unnaturally quiet and withdrawn.

He caught up with DeFalco.

"Ed, I want to talk to you a minute."

DeFalco stopped and took a cigarette out of an ornate case and tapped it against the back of his hand. He didn't meet Tanner's eyes.

"Something wrong?"

"Has Connell been saying anything?"

DeFalco lit up and fanned out a stream of smoke from his nostrils, smoke that was shredded by the cold wind. "Sure he has. You knew he would."

"Do you believe it?"

"No."

Tanner's voice shook. "I can't disprove it. For the same reason that I can't prove I have a bank account here or that I had a dental appointment yesterday afternoon or that every firm I've dealt with in the city no longer carries me on their books. Ed, I'm being isolated!"

DeFalco's face went perfectly blank. "What do you want me to do about it?" Tanner stared at him. DeFalco's face was cold and emotionless, the heavy black hair glistening in the dampness, strands of it moving slightly in the wind. A tense, powerful, handsome face—with the eyes of a man who was almost scared to death. "Sure, I believe you, Bill. Somebody's pulled your records. But how can *I* help?" He thumbed towards the hill behind them from which came the steady sounds of falling dirt. His voice was jerky. "Olson was curious, he knew too much. And look what the payoff was for him. I don't believe that a man just sits down and dies. Something got him. And something's after you. I don't want to be included in."

He dropped the butt on the ground and heeled it into the soft earth. His face was distorted in the half-light of the cold, cloudy morning, crawling with the vague shadows of the trees that flickered over it.

"I like this life. I even like it when it's cold and damp and when it rains. I want to live to be a very old man and sit before a fire and warm my feet and read the books in my library. I may hate your friend's guts but I don't want to fight him. I know I couldn't win." He stared off into the shadowed paths. "I wish you a lot of luck, Bill. I wish I had more guts but I don't. And I don't want to kid either you or me."

"You've changed a lot since Sunday night, haven't you?"

Something flared briefly in the dark eyes. "So I was sounding off. I was talking to hear myself talk. People do it all the time." He paused and took a deep breath, like a diver does before hitting the water. "I don't want to know too much about Olson. I don't want to know too much about you. I don't want to talk to you, I don't even want to be seen with you. You're a dead man, Tanner—and there's nothing that you or I or anybody else can do about it."

Tanner watched him get into his car and start off with a

roar, the wheels throwing gravel. DeFalco wasn't a coward. Sunday night he had been full of hatred and willing to eat fire.

But something had gotten to him.

He was driving the rented car back from the cemetery when he became gradually aware of somebody standing beneath an awning along the side of the street. He almost recognized the figure, yet couldn't place him. Somewhere, some place . . .

He just barely saw the little girl. He had a brief glimpse that for a moment froze the entire scene. The man beneath the awning of the florist shop, the few people standing in front of the stores, the flag in front of the post office hanging limply in the dampness, the police car double-parked halfway up the block.

And the five-year-old in the bright yellow dress dashing out in front of his car.

He slammed on the brakes and twisted frantically at the wheel. Then there was a sudden silence and the smell of scorched rubber and the cold feeling of sweat trickling down the nape of his neck. A second later he was out in the street, kneeling by a little girl who was miraculously unhurt, the tears of fright just beginning to well in her eyes. A crowd quickly gathered and then parted to let two policemen through.

"I wasn't going very fast, I was . . ."

They looked at him coldly.

"We hear that all the time, Mac. You guys drive through here like a bat out of hell and when somebody gets hurt—no, you weren't going fast! Me, I'm getting damn' sick and tired of it."

The other policeman turned to the little girl and bent down. "Were you hurt, Mary Anne? Did the car knock you down?"

She shook her head and started to cry. *"I want my ball! I was p-playing and it b-bounced away and . . ."*

The policeman made a face and put away his traffic book. "You're real lucky. If anything had happened to her we would have gotten your hide and tacked it to the stop light. Now take off and take it easy."

Tanner got back in his car and drove around the block and parked. He leaned his head on the wheel. He was still shaky, still confused as to what had happened. He had been driving down the street and the little girl had run out in front of his car. If he hadn't been lucky, and if he hadn't had quick reflexes . . .

But there was something more to it than that.

The man who had been standing beneath the florist-shop awning. A belted raincoat and a hat pulled low over his eyes so his face was in shadow. The same man who had been standing at the end of the pier when he had almost gone off?

Probably.

And the florist's little girl who had been playing out in front. Playing out of doors on a cold, raw day. And then she had had a sudden desire to run out into the middle of the street because she thought her ball had gone out there. And if he had been a shade of a second slower, she would have been dead.

And it was a near certainty that he would've ended up in jail, to rot there the rest of his life because release papers would be lost and people would have forgotten all about one William Tanner. They would have forgotten that he had ever existed.

One thing he was sure of. Little girls ordinarily didn't play outdoors on cold, raw days. And she hadn't run out into the street because her ball had actually gone out there. She had run out at the volition of . . . something . . . that had been standing beneath the awning, watching her and watching the street and waiting.

But it doesn't have to be any particular street, he thought. It could be a different street on another day. Maybe an old lady would wander out in front of his car, or a boy on a bicycle. The end result would be the same. The courts would do the dirty work and pull the chestnuts out of the fire for the Enemy.

He was being hunted and so far he had acted like a sitting duck. He hadn't fought back, he hadn't really tried. He had accepted the idea, like DeFalco had, that fighting was impossible and that he didn't have a chance.

But he wasn't entirely helpless. He knew that the man who was after him was the same man who had, somehow, killed John Olson. That it was one of those who had been at the meeting that fateful Saturday morning.

Which one?

He didn't know. But Olson had known. Somewhere in the past he had met the Enemy and had known him when he had seen him again. He hadn't been able to speak outright, but he had done his best to point the finger.

The answer to who the Enemy was, he was suddenly convinced, lay in Olson's own background.

And the place to begin was with Olson's home town.

7

THE train chugged into Brockton at six, Saturday morning, when the town was still up to its neck in nightgowns and bed sheets. It stopped briefly to pick up a dozen noisy milk cans and to drop off the newspapers and William Tanner.

He stood on the platform for a moment watching the train rattle away down the long stretch of track, then turned to the station. It was a one-story wooden structure with a sign in front saying BROCKTON in peeling, gothic letters. A note was tacked on the waiting-room door to the effect that the station didn't open until seven.

Apparently, when anybody left town, he thought, they had to leave on the evening train. He started walking into the village.

Brockton. It was a small town—probably not more than two thousand population. A grid of crisscrossing streets that ran for a few blocks, then faded into the prairie. Several blocks of business section and a local tavern with a broken neon sign swinging in the early-morning air and a whitewashed church with a steeple. A combination drug and hardware store with bamboo fishing poles leaning against the display window and a town hall that featured movies every Saturday and Sunday night.

Small town.

Farm town.

Backbone-of-America town where every politician wished he had been born. The town where John Olson had been born.

He checked in at a small, rambling hotel where the dust was thick on the leather-upholstered furniture in the lobby and where the bathroom was four doors down the hall. His room looked out on the main street. It was a large room, equipped with a brass bedstead and a gigantic oak bureau with a porcelain basin and pitcher on top. A glass wrapped in dusty cellophane stood next to the pitcher.

He hung up his coat and walked down the stairs to the hotel cafeteria which was, wonder of wonders, open for business. He ordered pancakes and coffee and watched the waitress as she walked back to the kitchen to fix them. She was young and eager to please—even at six-thirty in the morning—and bore a faint resemblance to the old man at the hotel desk. Probably a daughter or maybe even a granddaughter pressed into service.

The pancakes were thin and didn't soak up the syrup and the coffee was blistering hot and strong and remarkably good.

The girl stood behind the counter three stools down, idly polishing the marble top and watching him out of the corner of her eye. She was probably wondering just who he was and exactly what he was doing there, he thought. By noon everybody in town would know that a stranger had blown in.

"That's pretty good coffee."

She walked back, a little too quickly, and he couldn't help

smiling. The walk went with the pink piece of ribbon in her hair. What did they call it? Simple and unaffected?

"Dad orders it special—comes in every week on the train."

"Your father the man at the desk?"

She nodded. "He owns the hotel."

"Nice place."

She polished the counter some more and made too much work out of wiping the top of a ketchup bottle.

"You a salesman?"

He raised his eyebrows and she colored. "I didn't mean to be nosy. It's just that we're not exactly overrun with visitors out here."

"No, I'm not a salesman. I came here to see the Olson family."

She frowned and he knew she was trying to think of some way of asking him about it without trying to appear too curious.

"I knew their son at the university. He died last week and I've brought back his belongings." In a sense, it was exactly what he was doing. And it wouldn't hurt for the information to get around—people might be that much more informative.

"John Olson?"

"That's right."

She went back to the ketchup bottle. "I didn't know him very well. I guess I was only ten when he left town." She folded the rag to have a clean surface. "I'll bet Adam Hart will feel bad when he hears about it."

For a moment he felt like the coffee and the pancakes were going to come right back up. It took every bit of will power that he had to control the tremble of his hands.

"Who's Adam Hart?"

"Adam was a real good friend of Johnny's—they used to be together all the time. You know kids when they hero-worship somebody older than they are." She put the bar rag down and slid the ketchup bottle into place between the sugar bowl and the salt and pepper. "I didn't know Adam very well," she said slowly, looking down at the counter, "but he's the type you never forget. You could roll all the movie stars into one and they couldn't even begin to compare. I guess all the girls were crazy about him."

"Is he around town now?"

She shook her head. "Oh, no. Sooner or later almost everybody leaves Brockton. Adam left about eight years ago."

His meal was going to stay down after all, he thought. But for a moment she had really frightened him.

"This Hart fellow—what did he look like?"

Her face got pink. "Young, but not too young. Maybe twenty-five or so. Blond hair and tall and kind of thin so he looked like he was a little hungry all the time. Blue eyes and a smile that made the whole world bust right open. . . ."

She was serious, he thought, amazed. She hadn't known Hart very well but she had fallen in love with him when she was ten years old. What was more, she still hadn't shaken it.

She looked wistful. "You'd never forget him, mister. Once you saw him."

He finished his coffee and just sat there, staring at the nickel-plated faucets and the shining glasses and the little boxes of breakfast food stacked behind the counter.

You could eliminate Petey and Marge, he thought, Adam Hart was a man. Olson was dead and he sure as hell wasn't chasing himself. Which meant that Adam Hart *had* to be one of the five remaining men who had been at the meeting that Saturday morning. Even granting that it was eight years later, still . . .

But the man the waitress described didn't resemble any of them.

The Olson home was two doors down from where the paved street ended and three up from the encroaching prairie grasses. It was a small, white bungalow—too small and too new for a farm house—and Tanner guessed the Olsons had moved in recently.

He walked up the sidewalk, then hesitated a moment before knocking. It was still rather early in the morning. Maybe too early.

"You want something, mister?"

The man had come around the side of the house, carrying

a half-empty bag of grass seed under one arm. He was a tall, leathery-faced man with silvered hair half hidden beneath a dungaree cap. He reminded Tanner of the farmers who used to come to the stockyards with manure still clinging to their boots.

"I'm looking for the Olsons, but maybe it's too early."

The man spat. "Not too early, not by two hours. Used to get up at five when I had the farm. Still got a garden and don't see any reason why I should sleep late now." He looked sharply at Tanner. "I'm Mark Olson. You got something on your mind?"

Tanner nodded to the small suitcase he had brought along. "I'm from the university. I brought back some of John's things."

The old man opened the screen door. "Come on in, son. Mother's right in the living room."

It was dim on the inside, with the cool, musty smell that goes with a closed-up house. In the living room, Mrs. Olson was seated in a rocker by the picture window, a colored afghan tucked up around her fleshless limbs. Her face was furrowed and stitched with fine lines and her eyes sunken and dried.

She and her husband were about the same age, Tanner guessed. But her husband was still very much alive and she was close to dying; a worn-out, run-down clock, just waiting for the final, fatal loosening of the mainspring. She had no more interest in life than to sit in her rocker in front of the window and watch the winds dart through the prairie grass and the occasional visitor wander up the street.

"I'm from the university," he said softly. "I've brought back some of John's things."

She glanced at him and then turned back to the window, as if looking any place else but through the glass took too much effort.

"Patricia wired us that he died," she mumbled. "She said it was too late for us to go to the funeral. She said they buried him the same day."

Which hadn't been true at all, he thought. Then he looked again at the old lady and realized she would never have survived the trip.

"Johnny was a good boy," the old lady said weakly. "He

should have lived longer than he did. . . ." Her voice trailed off and her husband tugged at Tanner's sleeve. Tanner followed him to the small kitchen and took a seat by the table.

The old man was gruff. "You don't want to talk to Mother too long. She's been ailing these last few days. Johnny's dying hit her pretty hard."

"John was born here in Brockton, wasn't he, Mr. Olson? Born and brought up here?"

"Lived here all of his life until he went away to college. Maybe he shouldn't have gone. He came back one or twice in the summer and he wasn't the same. Kind of unhappy, kind of moody."

He set a battered, tin coffeepot on the stove and lit the burner with a match. His hand was shaking. "I always told Mother he was a farm boy, that he wasn't cut out for school in the city." His voice was low and close to cracking. "I'm going to miss that boy, mister. I never approved of his going to school but I set a lot in store by him just the same."

He was going to make it painful for the old man, Tanner thought. But it had to be done.

"His whole life was here, wasn't it? You know, his friends and relatives?"

"He had a lot of good friends." The old man went to the pantry to get some thick, china mugs. "Never forget one. Fellow named Hart. Adam Hart. Older than Johnny but I always thought the friendship was good for the boy. A youngster makes friends with an older man and he gets a better view of life."

The coffee was boiling but he made no move to take it off the stove.

"This Adam Hart—Johnny used to talk a lot about him," Tanner lied. "What sort of a fellow was he?"

"All man, son. Came from a gypsy family that had settled over on the west side of town. One of those families that has two dozen kids in the house and a trained bear in the back yard. The kids just couldn't keep away. No grass or flowers on the lot but some cherry trees the youngsters could climb. Johnny used to hang around over there. Adam was one of the gypsy boys, a lot older than Johnny. They took to each other and Adam used to help Johnny with his schoolwork and teach him how to play sports."

He got up and poured out thick, black coffee that smelled burnt and raw. "Adam will be real sorry to hear that Johnny's . . . dead." It took an effort for him to say the word and the coffeepot shook a little, spilling the hot liquid on the oilcloth.

But Adam Hart isn't sorry, Tanner thought. *Probably only a little regretful that he had to go to all that trouble to kill Olson.*

"Anybody know where Adam is now?"

"Nope. Nobody's heard from him since he left town."

"What did he look like?" The girl in the hotel restaurant had been pretty young when she had seen Hart. Her memory wouldn't be as good as the old man's.

"Early twenties—maybe just twenty. Light brown hair. About as tall as me, medium. Well-knit—he'd have been good behind a team of horses."

Tanner sipped his coffee.

The Adam Hart that the girl had described and the Adam Hart that the old man had known didn't sound at all like the same person.

Brockton High School looked a little larger than the town deserved. Tanner guessed it served half the county; the town of Brockton and the miles of farm land around it. The classrooms were deserted and for a moment he thought he was out of luck.

But the baseball coach, who was also the football coach and basketball coach and who taught swimming and track and algebra in his spare time, was still there. Coach Freudenthal was a chubby man in his middle forties with an easy, friendly air. He was working out in the gym, showing two twelve-year-olds how to shoot baskets. The backboards were old and the floor was warped but Tanner was willing to bet they still turned out championship teams.

He told the coach why he was there and the welcome smile slipped away.

"Sure, I remember Johnny. He was the star of the team when he played here. You would never have figured him for it, though." He turned to the boys and slapped the nearest on the rump. "Okay, kids, shower up and go on home." He started for his office. "How'd it happen, Professor?"

"His heart gave out. Overwork, I guess."

"That's funny, I never would have guessed he was a heart case." Freudenthal pulled off his sweatshirt and started rubbing down his paunch with a towel. "You know, you'd never have thought he was an athlete. He just didn't look the type, though let me tell you a lot of them don't. He just didn't have the build for it, but when it came to reflexes and a quick eye, I've never seen his equal. He won a letter in basketball." He slipped on a shirt and started buttoning it. "Maybe this sounds odd but I don't think he ever really enjoyed sports. He kind of drove himself to play them."

"Was he a good student?"

"One of the best. Just as reliable in his studies as he was on the basketball court." A smile flickered across his face. "Maybe he was more reliable. Johnny made a monkey out of me one night—he was really off. I couldn't figure it out, he couldn't even make a simple lay-up shot."

"When was that?"

"Don't remember exactly, sometime during the winter of his junior year—it was the same night the gypsies threw one of their big parties."

An alarm rang in Tanner's mind. "Did a fellow named Adam Hart ever go to school here?"

Freudenthal looked surprised. "Hart? Hell, none of the gypsy boys ever went to school. And just between you and me, I don't think they needed to. The closest Adam Hart ever came to going was when he used to come to watch Johnny play ball." He went over to the washbasin in the corner and doused his hair. "He was a pretty good friend of Johnny's, always on the sidelines cheering him on."

Except for one night when he couldn't make it, Tanner thought. *The night when Olson played such a miserable game.*

"Did John ever strike you as being the moody sort?"

"Not to start with. He was sort of a happy-go-lucky kid. You know how the pudgy type are—nothing ever worries them. He started to sober up towards the end of his junior year, got pretty gloomy. I remember I used to talk to him, try to snap him out of it. It didn't do much good. Something was eating him but I never had any idea of what it was."

"His folks say he didn't turn sour until he went off to college."

"You know how parents are, Professor. They're the last to know when something goes wrong with their kids."

Tanner got up to leave. "You wouldn't know if there are any pictures of Adam Hart around, would you? Any shots of the bleachers where he might have been in the background?"

"Try the *Eagle*. They'd have photographs if anybody would."

"Coach . . ." He hesitated. "What kind of a guy would you say he was?"

Freudenthal edged forward in his chair, his face glowing. "Do you know, I had another Thorpe or Mathias right at my fingertips, Professor. Honest, I mean it. Right at my fingertips. You should have met this Hart. He was a young sprout but he was one of those few people you meet and know that someday they're really going to be great. He could have been a great athlete. Hell, he could have been great in anything!"

"What'd he look like?"

"Late teens, give or take a year—right at the peak. Kind of a short fellow, dark hair, fairly bulky build. The perfect athletic type. Quiet. He usually didn't have much to say but when he did, it was worth listening to. Never put on airs, never dressed too sharp. One of the few young fellows you could relax with and talk to. Good head. Mighty good head."

The coach had described a third man, Tanner thought. Different from the girl in the cafeteria or Olson's father. The girl in the restaurant had seen the type of man that young girls always wanted to see in their dreams. Smiling, polite, a sharp dresser, a little on the thin and hungry side. Mark Olson had seen an unblemished Son of the Soil. Coach Freudenthal had seen the perfect athlete.

And everybody else in town had probably seen Hart in a slightly different light. Hart had been like a mirror, reflecting back what they had *wanted* to see.

Which meant that one member of his committee had left seven different impressions on the others. One member looked vastly different to each of the other seven. All he had to do . . .

Who am I kidding? Hart wouldn't leave such an obvious opening. He's masquerading and he'll do a good job of it, he's no amateur. I can bet my bottom dollar he looks the same to all of us.

But it would be interesting to see what Hart *actually* looked like. And the only way to find out would be to get hold of a photograph.

There weren't any.

The *Brockton Eagle* had no cut of Adam Hart, though the editor remembered him well enough and went on to describe a man who might have made the perfect country editor. Tanner went through the yellowing files of the newspaper and ran across a photograph or two where the caption listed Adam Hart in the background. But the photos were indistinct and blurry, as if the photographer's hand had jiggled at the precise moment he had taken the picture.

Adam Hart, apparently the best-known and the best-liked person in town, had been a nonentity as far as pictures went.

Tanner ate lunch back at the hotel and found out from the waitress that the Hart family home had burned to the ground years ago. Later in the afternoon he walked out to the west side of town to take a look at where it had been.

There was nothing there now but an empty lot, grown wild with prairie grass and ragweed and straggling bushes. There were a few cherry trees on the back of the lot and some stunted crab apple trees along one side.

He walked across the street and collared a neighbor who was repairing his front porch.

"The Hart home burned down eight years ago, mister. Just a few weeks after Adam left. Lucky he did, too, or he would have been burned to death with the rest of his family. Worst tragedy we ever had in this town. Old man Hart and his wife and all their kids and relations. Must've been close to fifteen— used every coffin we had."

The man drove another nail into a porch step. "Damned shame. Finest family I ever knew. Some say the bear got loose and knocked the connections off the gas tanks outside the kitchen. They shot the bear the same night; it was pretty badly burned, too."

"What time did it happen?"

"Late at night, a little after the evening train went through. People in the house panicked and couldn't unlock the front door, which didn't make sense because they weren't the type to lock up anything to begin with. But we found a lot of the bodies piled up behind it. They didn't have a chance. You know, one of those big wooden houses. Went up like a deck of celluloid cards—regular torch."

He straightened up and felt in his pockets for more nails. "It was a mighty big funeral. Everybody in town was there and Adam even got wind of it somehow and came back. Never saw a man so cut up, it really hit him." He tugged at his ear. "Guess it would have hit me, too, if I had lost my family like that. Never felt so sorry for a man in all my life. Believe me, Adam didn't deserve it. Never a straighter or more generous soul walked the face of the earth, let me tell you . . ."

Tanner cut him off with a curt "thanks" and headed back towards the hotel. It was near dusk, the sun sinking slowly behind the flat horizon of the endless prairies.

Brockton, he thought. A quiet little town with not too many houses and not too many people.

A little town that didn't realize it had spawned a monster.

He had supper and read for a while, then turned in. There wasn't too much more he could find out, he thought. He knew almost all there was to know about Adam Hart, even if he didn't know who Adam Hart was.

He stretched out and tucked his hands behind his head. He had come to Brockton to find out about John Olson but he had ended up finding out a lot more about Adam. And what really mattered, of course, was not the education of John Olson but the education of Adam Hart.

He could guess how it had all started. Adam Hart, a personable gypsy boy. Living in a house with a dozen other children, part of a family that kept a trained bear in the back yard and had cherry trees on the lot. Trees that could be climbed and had cherries to be eaten and there was nobody who would chase you away.

A mecca for every kid in town. And John Olson had been no exception. A pudgy little boy, happy-go-lucky and spirited, who hung around with the Hart children and ended up hero-worshipping Adam Hart. Hart's reaction? He had probably been flattered and somewhat amused. And maybe one day when Adam and John had wandered off fishing together, Adam made his big discovery. Maybe there had been vines overlooking the stream. . . .

Hart, athletic and with superhuman reflexes, might have swung across or climbed them and dared his younger companion to do the same. John, by himself, couldn't have done it. He didn't have the ability, he didn't have the sheer muscular strength. There had probably been a period of kidding and then John had tried, with Adam Hart, perhaps unconsciously, concentrating on the boy, unintentionally willing him to swing across.

John had done it. Maybe the next time, overconfident and with Hart not concentrating, he hadn't succeeded and had fallen into the stream. It must have set Hart to thinking.

And maybe Hart had suddenly realized that John *hadn't* made it across the river the first time. That it had been *he*, Adam Hart, who had made it. It had been John's body, but it had been Adam Hart's mind and nervous system. He had taken over John's mind and had pulled the strings that jerked the muscles and reflexes of his youthful puppet.

It must have been a wonderful feeling of power, Tanner thought. Adam Hart must have realized what he was then. That he was a superman.

It had probably been a lot of fun at first. Even John had probably gotten a kick out of it. He could play on the high-school teams and astound everybody with his ability. And Adam Hart must have enjoyed sitting on the sidelines, guiding John's mind so he could make intricate plays on the floor and shots that would make the spectators gasp.

Bu then there must have been a day when there was a split. When John Olson realized that he wasn't the master of his own soul, that he wasn't living his own life. He must have grown tired of it, must have wanted out.

But Adam Hart hadn't grown tired. John Olson was his creation, his puppet—the pet dog who had learned a hatful of tricks. And when his master wanted him to perform, John would perform, like it or not.

It must have been that which had crushed Olson. The knowledge that his life was not his own. That he had nothing to say about what he did. That Hart was master and he was something lower than a slave.

He felt a sudden surge of sympathy for Olson. It must have been killing knowledge. . . .

But Olson had finally gotten away. Eventually Hart had permitted him to flee away to college. And then, years later, Hart had shown up on the scene again. Olson had been terrified, knowing what might happen. That any moment Hart would pull the strings and once more he would be living the life of a marionette.

Tanner sat up in bed and took his pipe off the dresser. Olson had been added to the Project three months before his death. Had his nervousness actually dated from then? Probably. And if he had recognized Hart, why couldn't he simply have left? But maybe Hart had decided that Olson knew too much and he couldn't afford to have him leave.

Olson had tried to finger Hart, to point out that the Enemy existed and that something should be done. He hadn't been able to talk outright so he had . . .

Filled out the questionnaire himself. Deliberately phonied it to arouse the suspicions of the committee. And when that had failed he had seen his one chance start sliding down the drain and had desperately tried to argue it out. He had dared Hart. And Hart had taken him up on it.

But it doesn't fit, Tanner thought. *It was a stupid thing to do. And Hart is not a stupid man.*

Hart had known then that Olson would require constant watching and constant control. He had probably been standing outside the Van Zandt home, waiting in the dark, watching Olson move about his room, knowing that Olson had to die. John had come home at midnight and fought for three hours and finally broken the compulsion that had prevented him from talking or writing about Hart directly. He had sat down to write a letter and Hart had guessed what he was doing and killed him.

It couldn't have been difficult. Hart had known Olson's nervous system as well as his own. It would have been an easy thing to clamp down on it, to strangle the autonomic nervous system so that Olson's heart had simply ceased to beat.

And Olson hadn't been the only victim. Years before Hart had killed the people who had known him the best, who had probably guessed what he was.

His own family.

So one night he had come back. On the evening train. It had been a simple thing to let loose the trained bear and then stand behind a tree across the street and direct the animal towards the tanks of bottled gas outside the kitchen window.

Adam Hart, Tanner thought coldly.

The Enemy.

Adam Hart.

Monster!

* * *

It was a subtle awareness of other life in the room besides himself. An awareness of warmth, of movement . . .

Tanner jerked and rolled off one side of the bed. A moment later a figure was bending over the bed, pulling at something that it had jabbed through sheets and mattress to tangle in the springs. There was a brief moment of tense struggle and then the figure had the knife in his hands and was crouched, waiting for him.

He grabbed the pillow and used it as a shield when the figure lunged. The knife slashed through the pillow in a flurry of feathers and he felt a stinging in his cheek. Then he had the figure by the wrist and was bending it back to force the dropping of the knife.

The figure heeled him in the instep and he went down, still clutching grimly to the wrist that held the knife. They rolled against the bureau and he forced the wrist further back. A little more pressure and then a sudden crack and a thin, strangled scream of pain. They rolled once more, the figure trying to get its knees under his chest.

Then he had the knife and sent it skittering across the floor. When the figure started to scramble after it, he kicked it savagely in the groin. It doubled, moaning, and he yanked on the light chain.

A kid, he thought, *a young kid* . . . Maybe nineteen, maybe twenty. A farm youngster with clean-cut features and a hard, muscular frame and ingrained dirt under his nails and in the palms of his hands. Just a farm boy.

And a fanatic. Tanner felt clammy with sweat and sick with pain and excitement. "What were you after, boy? I haven't any money!"

The boy was in too much pain even to be sullen.

". . . didn't want your money."

"Then what were you after?"

The boy's lips started to tighten into a hard, thin line. He wasn't going to talk, Tanner thought, he wasn't going to say a word.

His own anger caught him by surprise. He grabbed the boy by the jacket collar and held him up so that his toes were almost off the floor.

"You going to tell me, son?"

The boy started to shake his head and Tanner exploded his other hand deep into the pit of the boy's stomach. The youth jackknifed and was abruptly sick. Tanner waited until the spasms had stopped and then lifted him again.

"Why were you trying to kill me?"

The boy didn't answer and Tanner slapped him, hard. Hard enough to make the boy stagger against the bedstead. It was making *him* sick as well, Tanner thought. *But a moment longer and I would have been sliced like an apple.*

"You going to tell me?" The boy shook his head and Tanner bit his lip and hit him once more. The boy doubled and dropped to the floor.

Tanner wiped his face with the back of his hand and swayed above the figure on the floor. He rolled the boy over with his foot and glared down at the blood-streaked face. His voice was low and flat. "I've been running for a week, son, and I'm tired. You either tell me why you were after me or I'll kill you and plead self-defense. You understand that?"

The boy looked up at him, dazed. "You were asking too many questions," he said in a choked voice. "You shouldn't have been asking questions about Adam Hart!"

"Did Hart send you?"

The boy nodded.

Tanner looked at him contemptuously. "What do you take me for? Adam Hart hasn't been in town for the last eight years!"

"He didn't send me after *you!*" the boy whispered. "And he didn't have to be in town—he told me eight years ago!"

Tanner stared at him, disbelieving, then got the picture. Adam Hart had been a cautious man. He had foreseen the possibility that some time in the future somebody might come back to his home town, looking for information.

So he had planted his booby traps, doing the delicate mental surgery that turned farm boys into deadly killers.

When they were triggered by somebody asking questions about Adam Hart.

8

THE doctor's name was Schwartz. He had rushed down to the clapboarded town hall which also served as a police station, took one startled look at Tanner and the boy who had tried to kill him, then hustled Tanner into a sideroom. He made him sit on the table, busied with his kit for a moment, then daubed at the dried blood on Tanner's cheek with cotton dampened in alcohol.

"Does that hurt?"

"What do you think?"

The doctor smiled faintly. "Doctors have a litany, just like priests; it's all part of the ritual." He went back to his kit and found a small hypodermic and a bottle. "I better freeze it for you. You make a face and it will be hard to sew."

A few moments later one side of Tanner's face felt pleasantly dull and numb. "Thanks for being considerate."

"Why not? You look like a cash customer."

"I take it you don't have many."

"I could use more. Too many people out here pay off in ham hocks and home canning." He was bending close to Tanner now, his fingers making expert passes with needle and surgical thread. "It was a knife, wasn't it? I don't think razors would be too popular in this town."

Tanner jerked a thumb towards the door. "The kid out there did it, in case you were wondering."

"So I gathered. He's Jim Hendricks—most people in town think he's a pretty good boy."

"He's very good. Particularly with a knife."

The doctor took two more stitches and coated the cut with salve and lightly taped a strip of gauze across it.

"Be careful not to smile or frown—at least for a few days. I wish I could say it wouldn't scar but it probably will. The cut went pretty deep."

Tanner could already feel the pain thread back into his cheek. The doctor started to wash up at a basin in the corner. "Are you going to push charges?"

"Wouldn't you?"

"Kids sometimes do funny things. I don't think most people out here would want to see a boy punished for the rest of his life for something he had done on the spur of the moment."

Tanner looked at him coldly. "Is that the way you look at it, Doctor?"

"No. But I'm afraid that's the way a jury out here would look at it. The Hendricks boy is well liked in town, his father's a respected member of the community—runs the feed store two blocks over." He pulled some paper towels out of a wall rack. "You've got to realize that you're a stranger. Country towns don't care for strangers, especially those from the city. Before the trial was half over the town would have convinced itself that it was all your fault. They'd probably twist it around so they could rack you on a contributing charge."

He crumpled up the paper towels and self-consciously potted them towards a wire wastebasket. "Why was Hendricks trying to kill you?"

Tanner's cheek had started to throb and he felt weak. He wanted to go back to his hotel and sleep for twenty-four hours, then light out for a town that had never heard of Adam Hart or John Olson. But he realized he wouldn't be permitted to do that. He was in the game all the way, and there was no getting out.

"Is it any business of yours?"

"No, but I can't help being curious. Things like this don't happen here very often."

It might be an act, Tanner thought. Doctor Schwartz could be another booby trap that Adam Hart had left behind.

"When did you start practice in this town, Doctor?"

Schwartz looked at him intently. "Five years ago. But it would make a difference if I had been here—oh, say for more than eight years, wouldn't it?"

Tanner said, "What do you know about him?"

Schwartz drummed his fingers on the table top. "I'm the only doctor in this town, I'm the only one they've had for the last five years. I know almost everything there is to know about everybody. I know all their virtues, I know all their sins. And believe me, both would fill a book."

He brushed the sweat from a faint moustache. "I never met Adam Hart but I'm surprised how much I know about him. He must have been quite a guy. He borrowed money from everybody but so far as I can discover, he never paid it back and nobody ever pressed him to repay. They wrote it off the books and considered it an honor. For kicks, he used to start fights among the young toughs in town just to see what would happen. Nobody ever complained. If anybody else had done it, they would have been run in. When Adam Hart did it, it was just high spirits.

"That isn't all. There were half a dozen bastard children in town at one time who could have claimed Adam Hart for a father."

Tanner felt a little sick, thinking of a future twenty years away when there would be six Adam Harts running around. "You said 'were'—what happened to them?"

"They were sickly kids—all of them. Nothing you could put your finger on, and nothing I could do for them. Maybe it was something in the genes, I don't know, but they caught every childhood disease there was and they didn't have any resistance. They died, all of them."

Unsuccessful sports, Tanner thought. Mutations that hadn't made the grade.

"The girls who had them didn't care that it was out of wedlock," Schwartz continued. "Neither did their parents. When Hart was younger he was precocious sexually and he experimented all over town—with everything and everybody. From the stories that went around, I can't think of anything he left out. In a medical book he would have taken up a full page in Latin. Nobody ever thought it might be wrong. For *him*."

Adam Hart had flagrantly and openly violated the taboos of human society, Tanner thought. And the members of that society had cheerfully forgiven him.

"As far as this town is concerned," Schwartz said in a low voice, "the only citizen it ever produced worth talking about is Adam Hart. Ever since he left, Brockton's been in an in-between state. It isn't living and it isn't dead. It's just waiting. There's a couple of other towns around here that are the same way, incidentally. Hart got around."

"What are they waiting for?"

"For Hart to come back, of course. And some day he will." Schwartz paused. "I sometimes wonder if Hart's been traveling around the country."

So a lot of other towns could get to know him, Tanner thought. It was something he hadn't thought of before. The whole country, waiting for Adam Hart to come back . . .

"You'd have your man on horseback then, wouldn't you?"

"That's right, you would."

Tanner slipped on his coat and started for the door.

Schwartz said, "What are you going to do when you find Hart, Professor?"

Tanner smiled faintly and the pain ticked back in his cheek. "Kill him."

At the door, Schwartz said, "Dr. Pierce—I bought his practice just before he retired—was always going to tell me about the Hart family."

"He never did, did he?"

"No. Six months after he retired, he had an accident. He fell down the cellar steps one night and broke his neck."

"You so sure it was an accident?"

Schwartz hesitated. "I guess not. But if I found out for sure that it wasn't, my life wouldn't be worth much, would it?"

Tanner nodded. "You're right, Doctor. It wouldn't."

9

HE caught the train out of Brockton early Sunday morning. There was no sense in staying to push his case. The boy was a home-grown product, and he was a stranger. And the local judge, a man who had held the office for the last twenty years, could hardly be expected to favor him.

Adam Hart took care of his own, he thought.

The endless prairies and the low blur on the horizon that had been Brockton gradually disappeared and he felt some of the tenseness drain out of him. In many ways it had been a smart idea going to Brockton. He had learned a lot about Hart.

And it had also been the sheerest luck that he had gotten away alive.

It was an uncomfortable thought. So far he had

made no move that Hart hadn't anticipated. It was still cat-and-mouse, with himself cast in the role of the mouse. Sooner or later Hart would tire of the play, the claws would flash out, and that would be that.

The train felt hot and uncomfortable and he made a half-unconscious gesture towards his collar. In the end it would be either the pier, or life as a living-dead man, like Olson had been. A marionette.

Now he wondered if Hart was after anybody else on the committee and if not, why not? What was so special about himself?

"Nice day today, isn't it?"

He glanced at his seat companion. A middle-aged woman, around forty-five or fifty, with graying hair and a face that wore its troubles like other women wore their lipstick. He grunted. She talked on in a sweet, determined voice.

"You get on at Brockton? That's a real nice town. Jess does his banking there. We've got a little farm not too far away. Do right well, though since we're country folks, we don't need much." She glanced sharply at him. "Were you in the service?"

"For a few years."

She opened her purse and dug down among the wadded handkerchiefs and the keys and the compact that leaked powder. The photograph she came up with was just what he had expected—the boyish face beneath the overseas cap, a half smile, and a carefully retouched glint in the eyes.

"My Ralph. He was wounded in Vietnam."

He didn't know what to say and she stuffed the photograph away, her doughy face starching itself into a someone-will-pay expression.

"We fought that war all for nothing. Never had the right leaders . . ." She paused and he wondered how political she was going to get. God, he hated the type. She snapped the purse shut like she was operating a guillotine and the flesh drew tight over her cheekbones. "What we need is a leader, a strong, honest-to-goodness leader. . . ."

A *leader*, he thought.

Someone like Adam Hart?

It had been practically axiomatic that the human race would hate anybody or anything that was superior to it. That it would do its best to destroy it.

But would it really?

There was the very possible chance that people would welcome Adam Hart with open arms. And why not? For the last thirty years people had done nothing but play follow the leader. They were broken in, they were ripe. People were worshippers by nature. They worshipped movie stars, they worshipped athletes, they worshipped dictators.

People wouldn't fight Adam Hart. They'd parade him down Broadway, they'd shower him with paper, they'd print his biography and buy millions of copies of it, every home would have his portrait.

What was it Marge had said?

I'm ready to build a little shrine in my living room just as soon as I know what to put in it.

"I've voted the straight ticket all my life. . . ." the woman was saying.

He sighed, bought himself a paper from the candy butcher and tried to bury himself in it. The same old news, he thought, blinking to keep awake. The same minor wars, the same tensions, the same murders and rapes and thefts—only the names had been changed, but not to protect the innocent.

Why did Adam Hart want anything to do with it?

And then he thought of the one person who might know, the innocent bystander who probably knew as much about Adam Hart as Olson himself. The one person who would know because she had been there. . . .

Olson's sister.

Petey.

He dozed during the afternoon, partly because he was tired and partly because he wanted to get away from the conversation of the woman next to him. He had supper in the crowded dining car, read a few optimistic articles in a professionally optimistic magazine, and was wide awake when the train came into Chicago. It was early evening and a light fog had rolled in from the lake so the city looked like a dark, gray mass of cotton, shot through with black shadows and with a million lights glowing from the depths—lights that were yellowed and diffused by the damp fog.

The train slowed and abruptly the gray night was replaced by the brilliance of the train shed. The aisles filled with people struggling into their coats and stretching to get down their luggage from the luggage racks. He tipped down a battered aluminum suitcase for his seat companion, then pulled down his own and sat back waiting for the aisle to clear.

Outside, baggage men were driving their small trucks past the slowly moving train, porters were waiting to step aboard to help old ladies with their luggage, and a hundred people lined the concrete platform waiting for Mom and Dad or Uncle Harry and Sister Ellen.

The line started moving down the aisle and Tanner watched the people on the platform greet those getting off. The car was half empty before he noticed the two men standing on the platform, a little to the rear of the pressing group of greeters. Two men in brown business suits and conservative ties and well-shined shoes who intently inspected everybody as they got off but greeted no one. They were waiting, he thought.

For whom?

Now the aisle was almost empty. The two men outside had moved closer to the stream of people getting off. At the far end of the coach, a colored woman started to sweep down.

The palms of his hands felt wet against the upholstered arms of his seat. He didn't know who they were or what they wanted but he was convinced it concerned him.

He made up his mind and ran to the opposite end of the car from the exit door.

"Hey, mistuh, you goin' de wrong way!"

He brushed past her and ran into the next empty car. At the far end, he worked frantically at the door away from the platform. It swung open and he dropped the few feet to the concrete rail bed, bending his legs slightly to take up the jar.

The shed was so damned bright. . . .

He stood there for a brief moment in an agony of indecision. His suitcase . . . his clothes and his service pistol . . . everything he owned . . . left behind. . . .

He started running down the tracks.

"Stop that man!"

A whistle split the air of the shed. The police, he thought chaotically. For some reason they were in on it. He frantically tried to run a broken field down the rail bed.

Spang!

Cement chipped from a nearby pillar and he doubled his speed, the cool night air burning his lungs. The concrete of the rail bed showered chips once more and then he was running in cinders and he was out of the train shed. For a brief moment he was silhouetted between the fog outside and the bright lights of the shed. Something tore into the fleshy part of his thigh, almost dropping him to his knees. He staggered, then the thin tendrils of fog floated between himself and the shed and he was plunging down a cindered embankment.

The gritty cinders shredded the skin in the palms of his hands and ground into the side of his pants where he slid. He ended in a tangle of weeds and saw grass and oily water at the bottom of the slope. He lay there a moment, shaking, the greasy water seeping through his coat and shirt and crawling down his chest.

I can run for it, he thought. But beyond the embankment there was only a well-lighted, broad avenue where he would make the perfect target.

He flattened himself out in the ditch. There were noises overhead and the slight rattle of rolling cinders as men walked along the rail bed ten feet above him. A flashlight cut through the fog and outlined a clump of ragged bushes two feet from his head. The light hovered for a second, then continued on down the track.

"I thought I saw him run on down . . ."

"Look for blood—I think I winged him."

"None here. This damned fog—he must've gone off the side some place."

The night was closing down and the fog was moving in thicker. The voices were a hundred yards down the track now but he knew in a moment they'd start back, watching the sides of the embankment. If he was going to leave, it would have to be now.

He got to his knees, wincing at the pain in his leg, and silently crawled the few yards to the sidewalk, taking advantage of the cover some bushes offered. The avenue beyond was a one-way street and cars were parked on the other side.

Forty feet of boulevard to cross, with no cover but the drifting fog.

He took off his shoes and felt around on the ground for a fair-sized stone. He threw it diagonally across the embankment so it clattered down the other side a good fifty feet from where he was.

"You hear it? Over here!"

"Where?"

"Down here—this side!"

The light bobbed towards him, then cut down the other side of the embankment. He stood up, crooking his arms so he held his shoes in front of him, and ran frantically across the street.

There was no sound but the soft slap of his stocking feet on the asphalt.

The cars, and then the blessed shadows . . . He turned south, to an alley, stopping for a moment in the darkness to wipe his hands on his trousers and probe the wound in his leg. A flesh wound that hurt like hell. He'd had a tetanus shot in preparation for the diggings in Colorado, but it would still have to be washed and bound.

He put on his shoes and cut through the alley for two blocks, then walked down to Madison Street. Skid Row, where nobody asked questions and where a man covered with blood and cinders wasn't worth phoning the police about. He sidled through a rundown bar to the stinking washroom, scraped most of the dirt off himself, and combed his hair. The wound would have to wait until later. Washing it would start the bleeding again and he couldn't travel through the city dripping blood.

He searched through his pockets. Half a dozen coins and a couple of bills and after that he'd have to pass the hat.

He walked back out to the bar and over to the phone booth. There was one person it was probably safe to call, though he couldn't expect much help. He dropped in a coin and dialed.

"Hello?"

He leaned close to the mouthpiece. "Eddy? This is Bill Tanner."

"Bill!" Deep silence for a moment. Too dead, as if somebody had put their hand over the mouthpiece. Then a jittery, almost hysterical, *"Long time no hear, pal. Where the hell are you?"*

"Why are the police after me, Eddy?"

"Police? You're kidding." Dead silence again, not quite muffling the sound of a door slamming. A screen door as somebody ran out to the neighbor's to make a phone call? *"What do you mean the police are after you?"* Pause. *"Where are you?"*

DeFalco had let him down at the funeral, he thought. Now he was turning him in.

"Bill? Something wrong? Why don't you answer? Bill? Where are you?"

He had maybe five minutes before they traced his call and the police arrived. Maybe a little more than that.

He quietly clicked down the receiver and dialed again.

"Marge?"

She knew his voice but she didn't hang up and she didn't scream bloody murder. *"I want you to know that I'm going to call the police just as soon as you're through talking."*

"Why are they after me, Marge?"

Her voice was dull. *"For murder."*

"Whose?"

"John Olson's."

"Do you believe I killed him?"

"I'm trying hard not to; I'm trying very hard."

There was a sharp click at the other end of the line.

Hart had sicced the police on him, he thought, shaken. It wouldn't have been difficult for Hart to forge evidence, to implant convictions that he had killed Olson. The rest of the committee members knew better but like DeFalco they had seen the handwriting on the wall and were scared to death. They were willing to go along, to throw him to the wolves. . . .

He left the tavern ten seconds before the sirens started to sound.

Chicago after midnight.

A million lights and a thousand voices along Randolph and State. Theaters and night clubs and drugstores and the open-all-night jewelry shops that specialized in zircons you couldn't tell from real diamonds. Couples heading home from the show and sixteen-year-old hoods on the corners, hair thick with Vaseline and combed straight back, their sport coats too long in the sleeves and too big in the shoulders. The life and lights and sounds of a city after dark . . .

Three blocks over, the concrete and marble cliff dwellings of La Salle Street, silent and dark with only the faint street lights filtering through the fog. The glass caves that looked with empty eyes at the deserted sound stages of the metropolis.

The lights marched out from the Loop along the empty streets, marking them with thin threads of luminescence that quilted the night into gigantic squares; the squares of a chessboard with himself pitted against the master player.

Some place in the darkness was Adam Hart, Tanner thought. Sleeping? Prowling the city? He wished he knew.

He stepped out into the street and hailed a cab.

Petey wasn't home.

He pressed the buzzer again, then walked over and tried the door leading to the apartments. It wasn't locked. The moisture and the heat of summer had swelled the wood so the door had caught without closing all the way. He went up the stairs to her apartment but he wasn't as lucky the second time.

He could wait until morning to see her, he thought—then realized he might not have until morning. And the empty apartment might tell him things that Petey wouldn't.

He tried the knife-blade routine between the door and the frame and discovered that the door had two locks, only the first of which was a spring arrangement. He glanced down the hall. It wasn't a new building. The wallpaper was discolored and the rose-figured rug was faded in spots and there was the indefinable odor of age. With luck, the building had probably been erected before the every-room-with-bath era.

He tried the apartment next door and managed to spring its lock. He waited a tense moment for noises from within—for the half-muffled voice, thick with sleep, to mumble, "*Who's there?*"

But there was no sound at all and he slipped quietly into the darkened room.

It was a bachelor-girl's apartment, dimly lit by light from the kitchenette. The sofa had been folded out into the bed and the covers were turned back, a pair of rumpled silk pajamas laid out on top. There was a faint noise coming from the kitchen that he hadn't heard before and he froze for a moment, listening. A radio, turned low, and a midnight disc-jockey show.

Nothing else. No sounds of anybody moving around out in the kitchen, no sounds of dishes clattering in the sink.

He walked quietly over and looked in. The icebox door was ajar, the makings of a sandwich on the table. There was bread, butter, lettuce, and a few slices of liver sausage. A half-glass of milk had been poured and he picked it up and sipped it.

Sour. The girl must have gone down to the delicatessen for another carton—and she'd be back any minute.

He went back to the living room, saw the door leading off of it, and tried it. The connecting bath.

He flicked on the light, then turned and locked the door he had just come through. He ran water into the bowl, let down his trousers, and sponged gingerly at the flesh wound. The caked blood washed away and the wound started to bleed again. He found gauze and tape in the cabinet and bound his leg tightly.

It wasn't until he put the tape back that he noticed what was wrong with the bathroom.

Face powder and talcum and bath salts and cologne and a fringe of nylons hanging from the towel racks. There was nothing unusual about it, not even the fact that the colognes and powders were of two different brands and the nylons of two different sizes. So two girls shared the same bathroom and had different tastes.

Except that Petey wasn't the cologne-and-powder type and she preferred lisle stockings to nylons.

He turned off the light and slipped into the other apartment. It took a moment for his eyes to get used to the dark and then he found a floor lamp and flicked on the night light set in the base—enough light to see the room with but not enough light to be seen from the street.

It looked pretty much like the apartment next door. Which was all wrong because there were too many details that didn't match up with Petey's character. The pink, tufted chenille bedspread—a little too frilly, a little too feminine for the grimly efficient machine he knew was his secretary. The same thing went for the curtains and the drapes.

For a brief second he thought he was in the wrong apartment, then saw a photograph of Petey on top of the dresser. A smiling, laughing Petey with her hair down and her teeth showing, keeping company with a table-top army of perfumes and lotions and lipsticks.

It didn't make sense. Petey wasn't the type.

He pulled open the dresser drawer and ran his hands through the garments in it. They matched the bottles on top. Feminine as all get-out. *What the hell*, he thought, *Petey doesn't make a practice of showing off her underwear anyway.* An efficient secretary with a grim exterior who probably liked to be feminine underneath.

The closet told him he was kidding himself. The suits and the cotton dresses and the drab wool ensembles were there, all right. But so were flowered prints and taffeta evening dresses and a black-lace creation with lots of skirt, no back, and a minimum of front.

Petey had been leading a double life, and nobody had suspected it. And then he wondered: *Why?*

There were muffled footsteps down the hall and the metallic jiggling of a key in the lock.

He turned off the night light and stepped back into the shadows of the closet.

She flicked on the ceiling light and closed the door behind her, then threw her wrap on the bed and stretched, shaking out her thick, brown hair and arching her neck. It was amazing what drab clothes and dresses had done, Tanner thought clinically. She had a figure and she knew how to dress it. And the way she moved. Not the sharp, awkward movements she used to make that made her seem like a cubist painting come to life, all squares and angles. . . . She was smooth, lithe, animalistic.

She had started to unloosen the straps on her high-heeled pumps when he said softly:

"Hello, Petey."

She froze for a second, balanced on one foot. "What are you doing here?"

"Just visiting." He took out his tobacco pouch and pipe. "You look pretty when you're all dressed up. Go dancing much?"

She kicked off the shoe and straightened up, one hand brushing back her long hair that had usually been worn in a bun at the back of her neck. "That's none of your business."

"So soon after your brother's death, too."

"You don't mourn a person forever."

"Not even for seven days?"

Her voice was ice. "I was your secretary at the university but you don't work there any more. And you've no right to pry into my private life."

He sat down on the bed and ran his hands over the sheets. Silk. You didn't buy silk sheets on a secretary's salary.

"Who replaced me, Petey?"

"Van Zandt, who did you think?" She deliberately turned away from him and walked over to the closet. She put her hands behind her back and unloosened the eyelets and stepped out of her dress. "Getting an eyeful, Professor? You don't seem like quite the rube you used to be."

Secretaries, he thought slowly, didn't buy slips of black nylon and lace on their salaries, either.

"Why didn't you tell your folks about John's death so they could have been there?"

"I told them later on. They couldn't have made it to the funeral anyway."

"Your father could have made it."

She glared at him. "You went up there?"

"I went through the whole town. I talked to everybody, from the little girl who waits behind the counter at the hotel to the math teacher who shows chubby little farm boys how to shoot baskets. They knew John very well. They knew Adam Hart, too."

"I don't know what you're talking about."

He smiled faintly. "Come off it, Petey. You gave yourself away the minute you stepped into this room."

She looked bored and started to roll down her stockings. "How?"

"I called up DeFalco and Marge when I came back. They knew the police were after me, they knew the police were convinced that I had murdered John. I don't think they believed it themselves but . . . something had scared them to the point where they were willing to throw me to the wolves. You're not scared, Petey. You're not scared at all. Because you're on pretty good terms with that 'something'? You not only know I didn't kill your brother, Petey, I think you know who did."

Coldly: "So what?"

That's right, he thought to himself. *So what? So her brother is dead and I stand a chance of being killed any day. And it wouldn't matter to her. It doesn't matter a damn whether I live or die. And it hasn't made any difference to her that her brother's been killed.*

The scene at the office and the scene at the cemetery had been part of an act.

He stood up and clutched at the sheet on the bed, his fingers clawing and bunching up the smooth, pink fabric. He yanked at it and the sound of ripping scissored through the room.

"Silk sheets—pretty expensive for a secretary, aren't they?" He strode over to the closet and ripped half a dozen dresses off their hangers and dumped them on the floor. "You were a great little kidder, weren't you, Petey? Good-looking girl and you managed to keep it hidden from all the boys, didn't you?" He brushed his arm over the dresser top and a dozen bottles cascaded to the floor. "But there was somebody you didn't hide it from, wasn't there? There was somebody you fixed yourself up for!"

"Get out of my room!"

He grabbed her by the shoulders, his hand sinking deep into her flesh, and shook her until her neck almost snapped. "Who's keeping you, Petey?"

Her voice was brittle. "Nobody's . . . keeping me!"

He slapped her so hard that for a moment he thought he had broken her cheekbone.

"You're a goddamned little liar, Petey. You're being kept and you're being kept by your brother's murderer—you're sleeping with Adam Hart!"

Her face was dull marble except for the mark of his hand that stood out in vivid red on her cheek.

"What do you want?"

"Who's Adam Hart?"

The strength had drained from her voice and it was shaking. "I won't tell you! I couldn't if I wanted to!"

"I could make you. I wouldn't hesitate."

"Big man!" she said bitterly. "If you think you can, go ahead and try it!"

He walked back to the bed and sat down on the torn sheets. He took a strip of cloth in each hand and pulled until it snapped. Adam Hart wouldn't have left himself open. Petey was probably telling the truth—she couldn't talk even if she wanted to.

"Why do you live with him, Petey?"

"Because I want to—what other answer did you expect?" Her voice became shrill and ugly. "You wouldn't understand me if I called you a small man, a little man, a weak man! You wouldn't understand me if I said you were *human*—and that explained it all!"

He looked up at her and felt dirty, as if he were still lying at the bottom of the embankment and the oily water were spreading across his skin again.

"Can you tell me what he looks like, Petey?"

She shook her head. "What good would it do? No two people see him the same."

"Could you describe everybody who was at the meeting that Saturday morning?"

She was sullen. "What do you want me to do, commit suicide?"

He changed the subject. "Do you think he loves you?"

She didn't answer.

"You must know that he doesn't give a damn for you. It's his own version of bestiality, only he hasn't any sense of morality to be outraged by it. You weren't the only woman—he's gone with others. Six girls back in Brockton had children by him. So you're pretty and charming. But your greatest asset is simply that you're handy."

"It doesn't make any difference to me."

He stared at her, trying to determine whether she really meant it. He finally decided that she did.

"What does he want, Petey?"

"How the hell do I know what he wants—he doesn't confide in me! Maybe he wants to run things, maybe he wants to run the world. Would that be bad? *We're* not doing such a red hot job of it."

"Adam's run things before. Your brother's life for one. And why? For kicks." He started pacing back and forth in front of the ruined bed. "Why are the police on my back?"

"You tried to call John the same night he was killed. They traced the call. And they found a note and some letters in your apartment. The police think that John had found out you were an imposter."

The records that had disappeared, he thought. The perfect setup. And it would have been easy to plant the note and the letters.

"Your Adam Hart's pretty bright, isn't he?"

She went back to undressing. "He'll do, Professor, he'll do!"

She called him back once before he got out the door. She was brown and ivory and brazen and something caught in his throat. Then he glanced at her face and her faint smile and her white teeth and the look in her green eyes and felt a little sick.

Her smile broadened viciously. "You know you're not going to live out the night, don't you?"

10

HE eased out the door and closed it quietly behind him. He didn't hate her, he couldn't hate her. She was just another puppet who danced to the piper's tune. But she didn't regret it, like John had.

He lit his pipe, flicked the dead match on the worn carpeting, and started for the hallway. Halfway down the hall, he stopped. The outside door to the apartments had opened and there were footsteps on the stairs.

Somebody coming home, he thought, little twinges of anxiety plucking at his mind. He listened. The footsteps passed the first-floor landing and went on to the second. And then to the third. A woman would have taken the elevator so it was probably a man. A man who was in a hurry. . . .

Then he knew who it was. He could *feel* him coming up the stairs, the way a swimmer feels the waves in a lake.

Adam Hart had probably been bored after he had dropped Petey off. A cup of coffee in a restaurant and then a sudden decision to pay Petey a surprise visit. A little sport before morning came.

Tanner stood in the hallway in almost fatal indecision, listening to the quiet footsteps and feeling the moisture starting out on his hands and face. He wanted to find out who Hart was but he had never meant to meet him face to face in a hallway. That kind of meeting could only end one way.

Now the footsteps were at the landing between the third and fourth floors. Calm, sure, and just a little hurried.

Adam Hart didn't know that he was there.

He hesitated one more second, then turned and fled down the hallway. Behind him, the footsteps on the stairs halted briefly, then bounded up.

who are you . . .

who are you . . .

who are you . . .

The end of the hall, a door, and a small red light burning above it. The fire escape and outside a clearing, cool evening with ten thousand stars spotted in the distant sky. A breeze that tugged at his collar and sifted through his hair, chilling the sweat on his face.

He could go over the side and four stories down to the blessed softness and safety of the concrete, he thought. No worries, no fears . . .

He clutched at the iron railing, suddenly panicky, then was running on the iron grid, spinning down the steel steps. Four flights of stairs taken two and three at a time. He stumbled and fell at the very bottom and for a second he was looking up at the building, staring at a shadow in a felt hat and a trench coat, silhouetted against the sky.

He got to his feet and started for the end of the alley, his legs shaking so badly he could hardly stand.

don't run . . .

don't run . . .

don't run . . .

His head suddenly ached and there were subtle probings, sudden pressures and jabs that brought sharp pain to his eyeballs and caused an uncontrollable itching of his skin. He opened his mouth to scream and laughter bubbled out instead, then his lungs suddenly refused to work and his left leg developed an involuntary limp.

A vague thought trickled through his mind. This was it. The master was learning how to pull the strings, like a violinist tuning his violin.

Then there was a sudden pressure on his heart, the feeling of a hand that was slowly squeezing it, choking the arteries and the veins and throttling the valves. The same thing that John Olson must have felt, although not as blessedly quick.

The alley exit was a dozen yards away. . . .

He fought back, trying to blank his mind, mentally grasping the fingers and trying to make them release, desperately trying to cause some pain in return. There was a brief hesitation, he took a quick strangled breath, and then the pressure was back.

The stars and the night and the cooling air . . . idiot laughter and curses and his own hands tearing at his chest, his eyes smarting and swelling.

Then he was out of the alley and on a residential street, for the moment out of sight. There was a sudden release, bafflement, and a frenzied groping in the air around him. His heels were a staccato echo on the sidewalk and he hurriedly switched to the dew-covered lawns. Far behind him, in the alley, there was the chatter of feet racing down the fire-escape steps.

He'd have to hide, and hide quickly. He couldn't outrun Hart and so soon as Hart had him in sight again . . .

He cut in towards one of the houses whose windows were dark and reflected the dull glow from the street light. A frame house which meant a back porch and . . .

The space beneath the porch was musty and thick with cobwebs. Planks and ladders and a lawn mower and garden tools had been stowed there. He lowered himself between two stacks of boards and shivered. He had been afraid and fear had pulled the strings as much as anything else. So damned, uncontrollably afraid. He forced himself to relax and to think of something else.

The musty smell of the rotting wood beneath the porch and outside a lukewarm night with the stars like crystal, inanimate ice in a pitch-black sky.

He waited.

The little things of the night. The soft noises from the trees and shrubs as small animals settled for slumber or foraged for food. The creeping things in the woodpile and the faraway echoes of automobiles two blocks over.

There was a scratching at the back fence and the gate creaked open. A boxer dog was framed in the opening for a minute, then trotted casually in. A swift inspection of the grounds, and back towards the garbage can just inside the fence. A nudge and a sudden clatter that filled the night.

If the dog came any closer . . . But it was pawing through the remains of an evening dinner and didn't wander over to the porch.

Then he felt a shadow in the yard and knew that Adam Hart had heard the noise and darted in to investigate. He could feel the cold gaze sweep around the moonlit yard, hesitating at the shadows of the rose bushes and the hollyhocks, lingering on the dim recesses beneath the porch. . . .

Be nothing, be nobody. . . .

He tried to develop a blank mind, a mind that didn't think of Adam Hart, that didn't think of being caught, that didn't think of hiding under the porch, under the porch, under the por . . .

Blankness.

Nothing.

A probing under the porch.

Nothing.

A gentle probing at the bushes and the shadows of the shrubs.

Nothing.

There was nothing in the yard but a boxer dog that had been worrying a paper sack of garbage and now looked up, wagging its stumpy tail. It forgot the garbage for a minute and started to trot across the yard, towards the shadowed figure that stood by the front gate.

And then there was *fury*.

The small noises in the bushes and under the porch suddenly died. There was an abrupt chittering in the oak tree and then silence. Something crashed down through the branches and thudded on the ground. The boxer growled and the hackles on its neck rose. It trotted stiffly forward, then suddenly froze in a patch of moonlight. It began to whimper.

Tanner watched, fascinated.

A muscle on the dog's left hind leg bunched and jerked and there was a brittle, snapping sound. He could see the muscles of the throat work as the boxer tried to howl, but not a sound came out.

Fury!

The end was quick. The dog's skin rippled and it went into convulsions, circling around its useless leg and frothing at the jaws. Suddenly there was a louder snap and it sagged, broken, to the ground. It jerked once, as if somebody had kicked it, and a growing depression showed faintly in its side. Blood gushed abruptly from the mouth and then the yard was still and empty.

Footsteps sounded faintly down the sidewalk. Then silence.

Tanner crawled out from under the porch. He glanced at the boxer, lying crushed in the middle of the yard, and imagined himself lying there. He stared, then went out the back gate and down the alley.

Clouds started to roll in from the west and the night air began to chill.

Downtown, the clock in front of Marshall Field's said one o'clock. The theater crowd filled the streets, heading for the IC station or waiting on the corners for the bus or thronging the restaurants that stayed open until the small hours of the morning.

People, the blessed people. He felt safe with them, with lots of them.

"Cuppa cawfee, mister?"

Dirty blue shirt and baggy khakis, a stained bristle of white whiskers and eyes that were all pupil and bloodshot lens. A shaking, outstretched hand with ingrained dirt in the palms and grubby fingernails.

Tanner started digging.

"I only need five dollars and thirty-six cents," the voice said hopelessly.

He pulled his hand out of his pocket as if he had been burned. There was nothing behind the bloodshot eyes, there was no indication that he was anything but a wino on the bum.

But five dollars and thirty-six cents was all the money that he had.

He stared at the bum for a moment, then whirled on his heel and walked away.

I can't go up to a policeman and say, "Officer, I'm being followed by somebody who isn't human." I can't vanish, I can't hide. It's out in the open. I'm the mouse and Hart is the cat. And may God have mercy on my soul for like Petey said, I shall not live through the night. . . .

There were couples walking slowly down the street, laughing and pressing close to each other. Two sailors stood beneath a dying movie marquee, looking professionally lonesome and eyeing the crowd as it swirled past. A matron, heels clicking loudly on the sidewalk, hurried towards the Grant Park underground garage. A group of soldiers talked in earnest voices to a girl in a doorway, the street light lost in the fuzzy sheen of too-blond hair.

The street was clearing for the short night.

He kept glancing in the store windows, trying to catch a glimpse of anybody who might be following him. Nobody for certain . . . and possibly everybody. He stopped for a moment longer, looking at the reflections in a Walgreen's drugstore window.

A glimpse of a man in a felt hat and trench coat? He couldn't be sure . . .

"I think that bird is real cute," a nasal voice said. "Look at him, that one there."

Pickup.

He glanced at the display. A little wooden bird teetered back and forth on a perch, then swung down to dip its bill in a glass of water. Up—back and forth, back and forth—and down again. No strings, no motor. Just the bird, its perch, and the glass of water.

"It's real cute. I'd like to . . ."

The bird lowered its beak into the water and didn't come up.

Five.

Ten.

Fifteen seconds.

Suddenly he knew what was coming but he couldn't turn away.

The bird swung up, winked a painted eye, and spewed a stream of water that splashed on the glass a foot away.

"Say, now wasn't that cute? How do you suppose . . ." Suddenly she decided it wasn't cute at all and started screaming.

"Somebody botherin' you, ma'm?"

The soldiers who had been talking to the girl down the street. They clustered around the window and Tanner edged away, not wanting any more trouble.

"He did it! He's the one!"

She pointed at him and one of the soldiers caught his arms and another hit him in the stomach. He doubled and tried to wrench an arm free. Then one of them slugged him in the face and he could feel the cartilage in his nose give. He went down.

Another soldier tipped his hat and took the girl by the elbow. "Just a cakewalkin' civilian, ma'm. No trouble at all."

Tanner shook his head and stumbled to his feet, feeling for a handkerchief to soak up the blood spurting from his nose. He was shaking with fury and started after the soldiers, then changed his mind and turned away.

He couldn't blame them. Adam Hart was actually throwing the punches. Adam Hart was working him over, trying to get even for his getting away the first time. Hart's human reactions, the curious mixture of man and superman. It was encouraging, if he could only live through it.

He walked aimlessly up Randolph Street, trying to keep with the crowds. A glance at the plastic soldiers on display in a toy shop window. Just a glance—long enough to see one of them present arms and to hear the tinny thudding of a miniature drum.

The night spots were winking out one by one. The actors were disappearing from the stage and he realized that soon there would be only he and Hart, alone on the boards and with no audience to see the final tragic act.

He wasn't aware, at first, of the old woman walking beside him. Her voice was a whispered croak.

"You don't want to stop Tomorrow, do you, sonny?"

There was nothing behind her eyes. Like there had been nothing behind the beggar's and nothing behind those of the soldiers who had slugged him. A certain vagueness, a certain blankness perhaps.

Just an old lady in black.

"Tomorrow belongs to those who own today, mother."

"Who owns today?" she asked sharply. "Not you."

"Who are you?"

"Do you think you'll ever find out?"

"Yes."

Shrill laughter boiled out of her withered throat. "Only if you live that long!"

She turned and walked away. When she disappeared around a corner he realized that he was absolutely alone.

Randolph, the other side of La Salle Street. The shadowed fronts of buildings, dead neon signs, and the indifferent glare of the street lamps. The still life of a sleeping city, broken only by the fluttering of a newspaper that lodged for a moment against a trash basket and then scuttled to a hiding place beneath a car.

He started walking again, then stopped.

Adam Hart was waiting for him at the end of the block.

A solitary figure in a slouch hat and a trench coat, the face, as always, in shadow.

Waiting for him to come closer.

He stared and the seconds ticked slowly by. He felt like a dog who had puddled on the carpet and was now going to be whipped by his master. He had a feeling something terrible was about to happen.

He tried to turn, to run.

He couldn't move a muscle. The man at the corner held him in the palm of his hand.

Then the fingers of the hand that held him slowly curled inwards and he stopped breathing, as abruptly as if somebody had closed a valve. His heart slowed and he suddenly lost all feeling in his legs. His hands went numb and the numbness sped up his arms, towards his chest.

Adam Hart was flicking off the switches one by one.

He was suddenly looking at a blackness far deeper than just the night and he could sense himself crumpling slowly to the sidewalk. He touched the concrete at the same time a police prowl car rounded the corner, the searchlight flashing in the doorways.

There was the squeal of brakes and simultaneously full release and a complete easing of tension.

"Hey, Mac, you can't sleep on the sidewalk here—sleep it off in the tank!" They helped him into the car.

The figure at the end of the block was gone.

11

HE was scared but he didn't go to pieces. He managed to lose his wallet between the car and the sergeant's desk so when they searched him down, they found no identification. There was nothing to associate him with the William Tanner who was wanted for murder. When they asked him his name and address, he gave them a phony name and an address on West Madison. They didn't even bother to check.

They threw him into the lockup for overnight and he thanked God for the crowded cell and the ravings of the drunks and the muttered, jumbled conversation of the others. He reveled in it for half an hour, then let himself lapse into a sound sleep. The ticking on his mattress was vermin-infested and his only pillow was his arm, but in the cell he was safe. The jam-packed jail and the confused mumble of thoughts were the best possible protection.

Heavy, steady slumber and then waking dreams that weren't dreams so much as a drowsy, mental review of what had happened. A kaleidoscope of shifting pictures, the main one of a man in a slouch hat and a trench coat.

He woke up shaking and biting his arm to keep from screaming. . . .

"Okay, let's get up! You bums can't sleep all day—let's shake a leg! Let's roll out!"

They gave him a breakfast of bread and cereal and let him bathe in a slimy shower room and shave with a razor whose blade was crusted with dried soap and whiskers. At nine o'clock they took him before the judge who yawned, looked bored, and since he was a first offender, let him off with a reprimand. By Monday noon they had turned him loose in the world again and he was on his own.

He stayed with the crowds on the sidewalk and didn't make the mistake of wandering into deserted sections of the public parks or venturing down streets that were empty of people. He headed back towards the Loop and the baking canyons between the steaming buildings.

Up Michigan Boulevard, thick with perspiring businessmen in wilted summer suits and women in thin, cotton dresses and a few sailors in baggy whites with sweat stains showing under their armpits. The lions in front of the Art Institute and the young saplings growing on the roof of the Grant Park garage . . .

He turned in at the public library, headed for the crowded newspaper room and read until noon. He had lunch, then found himself a bench in Grant Park, a stone's throw from Buckingham Fountain. Kids playing in the water, lovers on the other benches, a family having a picnic on the grass nearby. The safety of numbers.

Van Zandt.
Nordlund.
DeFalco.
Scott.

Grossman.

Which one?

Consider the superman: He toils not, neither does he spin. Or perhaps he spins too much. Given a superhuman needle in a five-straw haystack of humanity, how would you find him? He's a step up the evolutionary ladder, far superior to me and thee.

Of course—there's always one test which nature uses to judge new species.

Survival.

It might be as simple as that.

He counted the change in his pockets. Thirty-six cents. The five dollars he had had was still in his wallet and the wallet had been dropped in the gutter the day before and miles away. Thirty-six cents. Less than half a dollar to eat on and sleep on—or die on.

He wandered up North Clark Street and into a pawnshop, first glancing in the window to be sure there would be no other customer but himself.

"Something for you, sah?" The man was fat and oily and eager.

Tanner was noncommittal. "I don't think so, just looking around." The man's eyes flickered over him quickly, he was a little puzzled. The customer was worn and haggard but his suit was of good cloth and by the fit he had bought it new. . . .

"We've got some nice watches, really a bargain. Bulovas, Longines . . ."

"I'm interested in a pistol," Tanner said quietly. "Say something of medium caliber, not too big."

The man looked surprised, then reached into a showcase and laid a small automatic on the counter. "This is an Italian Beretta, really a beautiful gun." He hesitated. "You have a permit, of course."

"As a matter of fact, I don't. How much?"

"For you, a couple of hundred."

"That's rather high, isn't it?"

"Did I ask why you want to buy a gun without a permit?"

Before the owner could object, Tanner scooped up the gun and inspected it carefully. He flipped out the magazine then just as quickly put it back. "You make a habit of keeping these things loaded?"

The man behind the counter laughed nervously. "Of course not. We . . ."

Tanner leaned over the counter and pointed the Beretta at the fat man's stomach. "You did this one, uncle," he said dryly.

The man licked his lips. "You're kidding," he said flatly. "We never leave bullets in a gun."

"Don't you?"

The fat man's hand started to slide to a drawer just underneath the counter.

"I wouldn't," Tanner said in a quiet voice.

The pudgy hand retreated. "What do you want?"

"This gun, a box of shells, and say fifty dollars expense money. It's a bargain, uncle."

The fat man shrugged and handed over the shells and the money. Tanner backed away towards the door. He was in the doorway when the fat man cleared his throat painfully and asked, "Was it really loaded, Mac?"

"Like you said, uncle, you never leave bullets in a gun."

He ducked out, closing the door behind him so the fat man's string of curses was partly muffled. Down the alley to the next street over and he was in the clear.

A mirror in a restaurant window caught his eye and he stopped for a moment.

Not the neat Professor Tanner anymore, are you? Not the young, handsome instructor who sported a pipe and tweeds and a bright, intellectual glint in the eyes. You're looking a little seedy, Professor. Hair uncombed and a dirty, rumpled suit and clotted cuts on your face where the razor nicked you, and then the stitches Doc Schwartz took in Brockton. You're a little haggard and your eyes are a little red and some people might say you had a wild look. You've gone a long way— down.

The Van Buren Street subway station and the cool, cellar-like air, a welcome relief from the stifling heat outside. He pushed some coins through the wicket and walked down the stairs to the platform.

There was one thing he could do, he thought, and that was to start at the beginning. To go back to the university and the room where they had all met that Saturday morning. To refresh his memory and maybe find a clue that would help. But if he went back, he would be making himself bait. Summer school hadn't started yet, the campus would be deserted, and he would be alone.

He stood there and debated. Far down the track he could see the lights of a Howard Street train going north. He watched the lights grow bigger and finally made up his mind.

When the train left the station, he was on it.

The campus *was* deserted, the buildings gray and gloomy in the growing evening dusk. He worked his key in the door of the Science building and quietly slipped inside. The night watchman usually spent all night in a cubbyhole in the basement, reading thrillers and sitting with his ear glued to a blaring radio. He would be no trouble at all. . . .

He walked through the silent corridors and into the committee meeting room. The shadows were growing but there was enough light to make out the furniture and the worn marks in the tile floor. There was the long, heavily varnished table and the cheap, straight-backed chairs and the tinted photograph of an old professor, apple-cheeked and with mutton-chop whiskers, staring somberly down from the walls. Dust lay thick on the table and the window sills, marred by clean streaks where somebody had run his fingers or laid something down. And there were faint fingerprints in the dust on the molding and scratches around the door.

Somebody had gone over the room pretty thoroughly.

He stood there for a moment, wondering who it might have been and trying to concentrate on the mystery, rather than worry about his own exposed position.

Somebody coughed behind him and he whirled. He hadn't heard the door open, he hadn't heard the footsteps down the hall. But now Karl Grossman stood in the doorway, nervous and hesitant. Or was that a cover?

It is—I know it is!

Grossman started to waddle towards him, his hand outstretched.

"Professor Tanner! I . . ."

He let himself react automatically, not thinking at all, for thinking would tip his hand. The Beretta was in his hand and shots were splashing into the woodwork behind Grossman. He frantically worked the trigger, backing towards the window. He had a frozen picture of a shocked look on Grossman's fat face and then the big man was weaving towards him and had wrapped his cordlike arms around his knees.

It was like watching a slow-motion film where time had crawled to a halt and he could see each individual frame as it flicked past. There was no thought, no emotion, no feeling.

He felt himself go down, smashing a chair behind him. He tried to reverse the automatic, to bring the butt down on Grossman's skull. Then the physicist had his throat with one hand and was desperately straining for his gun hand with the other.

They rolled once and during the movement he worked the gun free and took hasty aim. Their bodies crashed into the wall and the thin molding near the ceiling gave way and the heavy photograph of the mutton-chopped professor plummeted down, at the same time the sharp crack of the Beretta filled the room.

Silence.

Smoke and blood and shards of glass. A frightened man on the floor beneath him, eyes glassy in a pasty face, stinking with the sweat of fear. But a man who was still very much alive. A man who wore crepe-soled shoes, so naturally he wouldn't have made any noise coming down the corridor. An average man who would have died if it hadn't been for the photograph that had shaken his aim. And it couldn't possibly have been planned that way. It had been sheer good fortune for both of them.

Luck. The only reason why Grossman had survived. Which meant that the physicist was . . . safe.

He took another look at Grossman and the blood trickling from a fragment of torn ear and got shakily to his feet.

"I'm sorry, Karl. God, I'm sorry!"

Grossman got up and fumbled for a cigarette. His hands were shaking badly. "I cannot blame you, William. I think I know what you have been going through."

Surprises. The world was full of them.

The chubby physicist gestured at the room. "I reran the experiment, without our people. I checked the room for little air currents. The tiny gap between the molding and the ceiling, any tiny hole in the wall, the little space between the door and the frame—everything. I assure you there was no way the paper umbrella could have moved. Normally." He paused. "And I know about you."

The pupils in Grossman's eyes were more their normal size now. He dabbed at his ear with a handkerchief, glanced at the blood stains, and shrugged. "I did some checking on you—for which, my apologies." His eyes narrowed. "It was very unusual. People who should know you claim you do not even exist."

"People like who?"

Grossman walked to the window and stared at the darkening campus outside. "Your banker, your lawyer, your doctor, your dentist. They have never heard of you. And you would be amazed at the number of students who remember the courses you taught—but not the professor who taught them."

Hart had been editing his past, Tanner thought. Rewriting his personal history so that he could be safely eliminated. Nobody would worry about him, nobody would be concerned. Because nobody would remember him.

"Did you find anybody at all who recalled me?"

"A few. The committee members, your secretary, and a Grandfather Santucci in Connecticut. And that was all."

"Did you talk to Harry Connell?"

"He does not remember you."

"He remembered me last Thursday."

Flatly: "Thursday was a lifetime away."

There were the sounds of footsteps running down the corridor. "Say, what's going on here?" The indignant face of the night watchman poked into the room. "I heard shots and it wasn't the radio. . . ." His eyes widened and he started to back out. "Mebbe I ought to call the cops. . . ."

Grossman took a bill from his wallet. "It was nothing, Joseph. Just a short talk."

The watchman hesitated, his eyes on Tanner, and Tanner could almost hear him wondering where he had seen Tanner before and why it was important to remember him.

Tanner sidled past. "Let's beat it, Karl."

It wasn't the night watchman that bothered him. It was the growing dusk and the stillness and the knowledge that they were alone and no match at all for other . . . visitors.

They took Grossman's car and Tanner slid behind the wheel. He drove slowly through the warm evening, going south again towards the Loop.

Grossman stirred uneasily beside him. "You know that the police are after you, William?"

"So I've heard." *Run, mouse, run!*

"I have done some investigating," Grossman continued. "I have not discovered much. You, I assume, have found out much more."

"You're taking your life in your hands if you listen to me, Karl."

"I have already taken my life in my hands. Tell me."

Tanner talked quietly, filling Grossman in on everything he had done since that Saturday morning—his own suspicions and minor triumphs and near death and above all, Adam Hart.

When he had finished, Grossman said, "We should tell the government. Right away."

"You'd have a tough time convincing them."

"I do not think so. A scientist could tell the government the moon was made of green cheese and they would call in a senator from Wisconsin to discuss tariffs. The government is willing to believe anything nowadays, William. It has to."

"You forget that I'm a discredited man, Karl. I'm wanted for murder. The government would spend all its time looking for me, not Adam Hart." Outside, the lights of wealthy Gold Coast apartment buildings winked quietly by. "Besides, call in an army of agents and sooner or later the news of what was going on would leak out. Then you could expect people to react one of two ways. They'd cheerfully welcome Hart as a dictator or else they'd start a pogrom where everybody of above-average IQ would have to run for their lives."

"What does he want, William?"

"I haven't got the answer to that one, Karl. Like Petey Olson once said, he doesn't confide in me." He circled a block and turned north on the Outer Drive. There was a full moon and Lake Michigan glittered with a soft phosphorescence. It gave him a morbid pleasure to watch dark waves roll in and then break in jeweled splendor against the long, stone breakwaters. The dirty city with a diamond lake front, the mink wrap covering the scrawny shoulders of a street urchin . . .

"Maybe he wants the world," Tanner said suddenly. "Petey implied as much. And for all we know, maybe he's well on the way to getting it. You read the newspapers and you can't help but think that the world is going to hell in a handcart. But maybe it's not going there under its own power, maybe somebody's pushing it. Every time a politician makes a big mistake, every time a scientist says something he shouldn't, every time a big wheel makes a decision that leaves the world in slightly worse shape that night than it was in the morning . . . how do we know the choice they made was their *own* idea?"

"But why would he do it?"

"Maybe it's because he's the first one, Karl. Maybe he thinks a little chaos will paralyze humanity so his own race can grow and thrive. Like the wasp's egg planted under the skin of a butterfly larva, where the egg hatches and the baby wasp consumes the living host."

The hum of the motor and the whirr of the wheels against

the concrete. The dark shadow of Grossman, slouched in his seat, his cigarette a tiny red flare in the blackness.

"You think about it too much and you can go crazy," Tanner continued. "I keep wondering *who* Adam Hart is and then sometimes I catch myself thinking it's more important to find out *what* he is. You know, the world has changed enormously in the last four thousand years. We're living in a technological age where anything and everything is possible and where just existing sometimes requires superhuman reasoning. But people themselves haven't changed much. Maybe now Nature intends to replace us with a new model, a race with a built-in hydromatic drive and power brakes, one that can live in a jazzed-up world without going off its rocker." He was silent for a moment. "I dunno—it was just a thought."

Grossman blew smoke against the windshield. "What do you think of Herr Hart—personally?"

It shook him up for a moment. What *did* he think of Hart? What did he *really* think? He had been too busy running to actually give it much thought. . . .

"I suppose I don't hate him—in an abstract sense. Maybe he *could* do a better job of running things than human beings could. If he wanted to. At least, he would probably see that we were well taken care of. As well fed and sheltered as a farmer's cattle."

Outside, the silent city and the bright-eyed automobile bugs gliding quietly down the Drive.

"Do you think, William, that the cows would have an opportunity to set up a union?"

Tanner didn't answer.

"It's getting late," Grossman said. "Maybe we should go home."

"Yours?"

"You have no place else to stay, have you?"

"You don't think Anna will object?"

"Anna will do as I say, William."

"You know this is a dangerous thing for you to do, don't you, Karl?"

"So? I do not care to stand by and watch this thing happen."

"Is your house being watched?"

"I do not think so—and I have tried to make very sure."

Tanner felt like laughing. How sure was sure? He turned off on a side street and concentrated on watching the street signs so he wouldn't miss Grossman's house. But in the back of his mind there was a slight, nagging doubt. He had talked a lot to Karl because he considered Karl safe. But no matter what test he ever devised for Karl and the others, he could never really be certain that Karl was really . . .

Karl.

12

IT was late Monday evening but not everybody had gone to bed. The weather was hot and sticky and he could feel the electric uneasiness that preceded a thunderstorm. There was the low jumble of voices from people rocking on their front porches and the whispers of those sprawled out on the grass, staring at the stars and praying for cool air.

He parked in front of Grossman's home. The physicist opened the door and led the way to the large, fragrant kitchen.

"Anna and the boys must be in bed, so we will be quiet. But maybe a glass of beer and a sandwich would go good, eh?"

He nodded and Grossman opened the refrigerator

door and set dishes out on the table. "We have salami and wurst and some good American cheese—try it on the pumpernickle. Cold beef and mustard and . . . William, have you ever tried this creamcheese cake?"

"With beer?"

"It is not so bad as you think." Still looking in the box, Grossman tried to set the plate on the table. He didn't quite make it and the sound of china shattering on the linoleum was loud and ugly. He held up his hands. "Anna will wake up now but she does not mind a snack at night." He winked. "I do not think she will be too angry."

Tanner started to butter a slice of bread. "I'll make up a sandwich for her—pour a little oil on the troubled waters."

A light clicked on in a room down the hall and there was the sound of slippers padding heavily on the worn carpeting. Anna Grossman waddled into the patch of light in the kitchen doorway, her heavy features still thick with sleep.

Grossman closed the icebox door and turned towards her. "I have brought home Professor Tanner, Anna. He will be staying with us for the night." He smiled and nudged a chair with his foot. "We were thinking we would have a little something before turning in and . . ."

His smile faded. The heavy, stolid expression on Anna's face hadn't changed. There was no welcoming smile, no angry frown, no look of recognition written there at all.

"What are you doing in my house?"

Grossman looked a little grim. "I did not mean to waken you, Anna, but in any case we do not argue in front of guests."

"What are you doing in my house?"

"Anna! As your husband, I command . . ."

"My husband died five years ago!"

Tanner stepped forward. "Don't you remember me, Mrs. Grossman?"

Her eyes flicked at him coldly. "I have never seen either one of you before in my life. Now get out of here before I call the police!"

Grossman was breathing heavily. *"Rudolph! Frederick!"*

There was an immediate scurrying down the hall and two sturdy boys about twelve years old popped into the kitchen. "Your mother is sick—you will take her to her room."

They edged back towards their mother, hostility etched deep in their faces. They didn't recognize Grossman either, Tanner thought. Hart must have found out that the physicist was doing some investigating. And now Karl was going to pay the price.

Grossman started to crumble. "Anna, I—I do not understand. I am your *husband!* I . . ." The stern expression on her face didn't change and he turned to the boys. "You know your own father, boys. . . ."

"Pop died a long time ago," one of the boys said coldly. "He got killed in a car accident."

Anna Grossman threw open the kitchen door. "Frederick, go next door and get help! Rudolph, call the police!"

The neighbors wouldn't remember either, Tanner thought. It wasn't going to do any good to stay and try and bluff it out, the neighbors would hold them until the police arrived and then the fat would really be in the fire. He'd be racked on a murder charge and they'd get Karl on a charge of breaking and entering.

"Come on, Karl," he said gently. "Let's go."

The big man slumped in a chair. "My family—I have lost my family!"

Tanner grabbed him by the shoulders and shook him savagely. "They're not going to remember you, Karl, no matter what! Hart's made you pay and if you stay here you'll be playing right into his hands!" He turned and started running towards the front door. Whether Grossman followed him or not was up to the physicist. But he could hear loud voices next door and he knew that this was his last chance to leave.

There were footsteps behind him and when he got into the car, Grossman slid in beside him. The lights were on in the houses on either side of Grossman's home and two men had started running towards the car. He gunned the motor and they roared away.

He drove for a few minutes and then glanced casually at the quiet shadow sitting next to him.

Before, Grossman had always impressed him as being a big man, fat but with a thick layer of muscle beneath it. Now Grossman suddenly struck him as being small and pudgy and weak and curiously empty. Like a paper milk carton, firm and solid when it was full, and light and flimsy and easily crushed when the milk had been poured out.

Adam Hart had won another round.

Midnight, Monday, and the rain had started to pelt down, huge drops that mixed with the dust on the windshield and made oily smears that the wiper couldn't get rid of. It had been an hour since Grossman had had anything to say and Tanner hadn't prompted him. They had driven around the city and he had let the scientist talk when he wanted to and had kept his own mouth shut when he hadn't wanted to.

"William? You have not asked me why I am willing to help you."

"That seems rather obvious."

"It is not entirely because of Anna or the boys."

Tanner didn't say anything. The only thing that would help would be to let Grossman talk it out.

"Have you ever seen a water dowser, William?"

"I once had an uncle who claimed he could dowse for water."

"That is something most people do not believe in. But I saw it done once, a long, long time ago, when I was a young man and had just come over to this country. I worked in Nevada for a year and there was a man in town who made a living that way. It worked. The willow twig actually moved and when they dug, they found water. And do you know what I thought, William?"

"No, I don't, Karl."

Grossman cranked the window down a little and let the wet wind blow through the car. "I thought of all the poor fools that did not have the talent to dowse and had to go out and make their mistakes and perhaps dig dry holes and do a lot of work before they found it." He was silent for a moment. "I want to help you, William, primarily because I do not want to see the poor fools kicked out and the world turned over to the water dowsers."

They drove in silence for a few more miles, then Grossman said, "You have a plan?"

"That's right, Karl. I've got a plan. Our problem is one of survival. We've got to smoke Hart out, to threaten his survival. To place him in a situation where his own reactions will be the tipoff, where he'll *have* to show himself to get out. Like I did with you this afternoon. Only that time the results were unintentional." He took a deep breath. "I'm going to try and kill each member of the committee, Karl. When I do not succeed— that will be the tip-off."

"But that is murder!"

"Not exactly. The situation is in two parts. My part is to try and kill the suspected party. I make my plans, there is no backing out, and I will not be able to stop halfway. If Hart read my mind, he would read only murder. I'll set up the situation and then tell you what it is. It's up to you to solve it, to stop it at the last minute. But you'll never tell me the solution, I'll never know it."

"And what is to stop Adam from reading your mind and knowing it is a false situation?"

"Perhaps he could, but he couldn't read the solution. It would still be up to him to get out of it, unless he had absolute faith in your ability to prevent it. And I doubt that an organism keyed to survival would have that faith."

"And what of my own mind?"

"I'm gambling on the element of surprise. The chances are he would be far too busy concentrating on the threat at that precise moment to pay too much attention to you."

A little of Grossman's strength had flowed back into him, a little of the milk had been poured back into the carton. He turned the idea over in his mind and Tanner could sense Grossman's intensely logical brain examining it from every angle. "It is rather risky."

"I can't deny that."

"And if you or I should slip in the case of an innocent person?"

"Then we're murderers."

He drove back into Chicago and the Near North Side, looking for a cheap hotel to spend the night. Before they turned in, Grossman said, "When you find out who Adam Hart is, William, what do you intend to do about it?"

He was surprised at how readily his own answer came. "Kill him, of course. And if I don't succeed, I'll shout his identity from the roof tops. Some place, Karl, somebody will believe me. Maybe two or three, maybe more. The story will spread and I think that will be the beginning of the end of Mr. Adam Hart."

They went up to the room and he flicked off the lights and placed a chair to one side of the window. "You want the first shift, Karl? Four hours on, four hours off. I think you'll have a warning if . . . anything . . . tries to reach you. Wake me up immediately."

Grossman took the Beretta and sat in the chair. "Who do we try first tomorrow?"

The first guinea pig, the first one they would eliminate. . . . He picked one out of thin air. "Professor Scott. He could help us quite a bit on the rest, once he's eliminated."

He got into bed and tried to push a thought into the back of his mind, the nagging thought that kept reminding him he could never quite be sure of Karl, or of anybody else. Just before he dozed off, Grossman stirred in his chair by the window and said:

"You know, William, I do not think we will succeed. We are too much like dogs—plotting to capture the dog catcher."

13

PROFESSOR *Scott.*

A seventy-year-old eccentric who wakes at eight in the morning, when the sun strikes through the bedroom window and lances across the thin blankets he uses even in the summertime.

He gets up and dresses slowly; his underwear drapes loosely on his bony hips. He'd be the last to admit it but morning is hard on him and he sits on the edge of the bed a minute to build up his strength. Then he walks into the bathroom and lathers the weathered angles of his face with a brush that smells of rot and has lost half its bristles. His razor is an old-fashioned straight-edge. The flashing metal shakes momentarily in his hand, then steadies when he brings it into contact with his face.

He shaves and finishes dressing and toys with the simple

breakfast the housekeeper has prepared—flaccid oatmeal and toast spread with marmalade. He spends an hour with the morning paper; his mind is still keen and it's only occasionally he forgets a story five minutes after reading it. Then it's slowly out the door for a short walk in the park, where he will relax on a bench and soak up the sunshine and speculate with humor on the shortcomings of the younger generation.

A vigorous man growing old, sitting in the sun and watching the days flick by, thinking each morning is just a little chillier than the one before, that each walk to the park takes just a little more out of him.

Or is it all an elaborate front designed to fool the peasants?

Tanner stretched uneasily behind the wheel of the car.

Did Scott actually bound out of bed with the reflexes of a thirty-year-old, run an electric razor around his jaw, take a needle-spray shower, and then settle down to a breakfast of sausage and fried eggs and steaming black coffee? Had the housekeeper been . . . indoctrinated . . . so she wouldn't tell? When Professor Scott creaked down the front steps was it just Adam Hart mimicking the actions of an old man?

It was possible. But then anything was possible.

It was a scorching day, the sun a blazing plate in the clear blue sky. The kind of day when the firemen open the hydrants and the asphalt feels sticky and a lawn can turn from green to brown between sunrise and sunset. It was midafternoon and most people were down by the beach, or trying to sleep off the heat in sweat-soaked hammocks and porch swings.

The curving walks in the park were almost empty. A little boy, his short pants soaking wet, was playing with the drinking fountain, holding his thumb over the spout and seeing how far the squirting water would go. A couple were on the tennis courts, the *thunk* of the ball against the racket breaking the puddling stillness of the afternoon.

And there was an old man walking slowly past the empty benches, searching for one in the shade.

Professor Scott.

The old suit that was just a shade too big now, a straw hat, and a rolled-up copy of the paper under his arm. His back a little hunched with age, his walk a tired imitation of his once-jaunty stride.

An act?

Tanner turned the key in the ignition and started the car. Professor Scott wouldn't find a shady bench on that side of the street; his favorite spot was in the full glare of the sun, the wooden seats and the metal armrests too hot to be comfortable. Sooner or later the old man would have to cross over.

And when he did, the moment of decision would be upon him.

The old man suddenly stopped and glanced towards a shady spot under the trees, a dozen yards away, on the same side of the street. Tanner held his breath. Scott *had* to cross the street; if he didn't, it would be all off. The plan wouldn't work later in the day, the park would be too crowded.

Professor Scott obligingly continued straight ahead.

Tanner felt a little sick and nervous. He eased the car away from the curb and let it glide slowly down the tarry street that paralleled the sidewalk. The essential element of surprise. Professor Scott didn't know what was going to happen—and neither did Adam Hart.

But he shouldn't think about it. That would be dangerous.

Action.

Blankness.

A few feet more and the sidewalk ended at an intersection. Beyond the junction there was only one walk and that was on the opposite side of the street.

He leaned heavily on the accelerator and glanced quickly around. The empty park and the deserted benches, the little boy at the fountain and the tennis players hidden from view by a curve in the road.

No witnesses.

Professor Scott was stepping off the curb, preparing to cross the intersection at a diagonal.

Sweat was making the palms of his hands slippery against the plastic steering wheel. The car was leaping down the street now, its engine roaring in the quiet afternoon.

The old man had stopped and was looking up, startled.

The perfect target:

One slip and I'm a murderer, Tanner thought. *But it's too late now to stop. I couldn't stop if I wanted. Grossman . . . But I mustn't think. . . .*

Professor Scott was turning to run, his face a mask of fear. He had dropped his paper and his straw hat had fallen off and was rolling into the gutter.

Let's see you change now, Professor! If you're Hart then you're off balance, there's nothing you can do to stop this car. Let's see you suddenly leap for the curb, let's see you sprint down the street with a thirty-year-old's muscles. And if you do then it's going to be all over. You'll have lost the game! But if you can't run faster than a hobble, then please God let Grossman do his share. . . .

And then it occurred to him that if Scott was really Scott, he could just as easily die of heart failure from fright or overexertion. Sudden panic clutched him by the throat.

He was in the intersection now. Professor Scott was past it but still in the middle of the street, his legs working frantically. *Oh God . . .*

He was a split second from murder. Then a blue sedan shot out of the intersection and smashed into his trunk. There was the squeal of tires and the scream of tearing metal and then the impact threw the two cars together like the arms of a collapsing V. His car jumped the curb and rocked to a rest.

The sun and the heat and a moment of startled quiet. He frantically worked the door handle, then put his shoulder against the panel and forced it open. A huddled form lay in the street fifty yards away. They were off to a great start, he thought. They had wrecked two stolen cars and nearly killed a man.

But the problem of who was Adam Hart had been decreased by a factor of one.

Grossman got out of the blue sedan and hurried over. "William, is he . . ."

"No, probably just fainted. Give me a hand here."

"All right, but I think we . . . Watch out!"

The truck was speeding and Tanner got out of the way just in time. Then he realized it wasn't after either him or Grossman, that somebody else had been the target for the day. It could have missed the fallen form of Professor Scott; it actually had to swerve out of its way to hit him.

There was a *thunk* and a tearing sound and then the truck had disappeared around the curve.

A block away, there was a sudden babble of voices.

Grossman's face was starchy white. "It could have missed him!"

Tanner raced up to the bleeding figure. He took one look and knew there was nothing anybody could do for the old man. He knelt down and hurriedly searched through the torn pockets, found what he wanted, and scrambled for the shrubbery lining the road.

Grossman was close behind him. "What are you doing?"

"Getting out of here. How much luck do you think we would have convincing a crowd that we hadn't run over the old man? With Hart around to whip them up, we'd be lucky if we didn't end up dangling from a tree. Where'd you leave your own car?"

"A business street a few blocks from here. Where are we going?"

"To Professor Scott's home—before the police get there. The old man was killed for more reasons than just to make us look bad. I want to find out why!"

A crowd had begun to gather around Scott's body but by then they were out of sight. In a drugstore Tanner made a phone call to Scott's home. He passed himself off as a police officer and told the housekeeper what had happened and that she should get there as soon as possible.

Then he drove around to the house and parked until she had left. He took out of his pocket the things he had taken from the dead man's clothing and started to sort through them.

Grossman looked at him accusingly. "Why did you take his wallet?"

"Because money isn't going to do Professor Scott any more

good. But it might come in very handy for us for such little things like eating and hotel rooms, or hadn't you thought of that?" He brushed his hand across his forehead. "I'm sorry, Karl, I'm a little jumpy. Let's go in."

He opened the door with the keys he had taken from Scott's body. The house was lavender and old lace with antique furniture made of thick cherry wood, hand-turned. A family album was on the sideboard, along with a chest of silver that was stained and tarnished. In the bedroom there was a tintype on the dresser and an old shaving mug whose gold letters had been nearly worn away. The room was closed up and stuffy and there was dust and yellowed curtains and the stink of age.

He rifled quickly through the dresser drawers and went hurriedly through the clothes in the closet. One suit caught his eye and he laid it aside on the bed. Scott had been a withered old man but he had a large frame. The suit would fit him, Tanner thought, and Lord only knew he needed a new one.

Grossman was leery. "His suit, too, William?"

"The dead don't give a damn, Karl, and I need one."

"You are looking for something?"

"Yeah, but I'm not sure what. Some note, some message. Something that would have made it dangerous for Scott to live any longer."

"Perhaps he had a den?"

He hadn't seen any on the main floor but it was logical that Scott would have had some kind of a workroom. He snapped his fingers. "Let's try the basement."

At first glance the basement was like any other basement. An oil furnace and a washing machine and dryer and the screens stacked up in one corner. There was a room just off the side and he stepped in and flipped the light switch.

The lights were fluorescent and it took a moment for them to come on. It was different than he had expected and a good deal different from the upstairs of the house. The study was a modernistic room with pine paneling and a mobile hanging from the ceiling at one end. Shelves of books were built right into the wall and one whole wall was devoted to a battery of filing cabinets.

He didn't know where to start. He didn't know what he could expect to find, he wasn't even sure of what he was looking for. He looked over the den carefully, then two things caught his eye.

The first was a file card on the desk with a heading neatly typed on it reading: "Heterosis, bibliography." On the card, Scott had written: *"The most important. See dossiers."*

What dossiers? he thought.

And on whom?

And then he knew. Professor Scott had moved fast, possibly even faster than Hart had. The old man hadn't lost any time. He had started assembling a dossier on each member of the committee before people had started to . . . forget.

But where would the dossiers be?

He looked through the desk and the bookcases, then came back to the shelf above the desk itself. An open space, about two inches, in the middle of the small group of books. Just right for half a dozen eight-by-twelve file folders.

Somebody had taken them, somebody who had entered the house about the same time Professor Scott had left for his walk in the park. Somebody who had known about the dossiers or had suspected their existence.

Who?

The other item depressed him. Scott had had access to the same information about John Olson that he had had and the old man had looked up a medical directory and then written a letter to Brockton. It was addressed to *Dr. Herman Schwartz, Brockton, South Dakota.*

It had come back, stamped:

Deceased.

The return postmark was Sunday night.

Saturday evening he had talked to Schwartz, he thought. Either he had unintentionally given Schwartz away or else . . . He looked at the back of the envelope. Somebody had read it and resealed it and they hadn't done a good job. The chances were that Schwartz had never received the letter, a letter that undoubtedly asked questions about Adam Hart. Somebody who worked in the post office automatically read the incoming mail so any information relating to Adam Hart could be sidetracked and destroyed, and the people to whom it was sent could be investigated.

Schwartz had guessed that his life might not be worth a plugged nickel. And how right he had been.

He shivered. The pleasant little town of Brockton dozing under the South Dakota sun. Nice, friendly people who would be glad to pass the time of day with you and talk to you about their kids and what went into Mrs. Whosis' angel-food cake. But for anybody who wanted to ask questions about Adam Hart, the town was a death trap, a multipetaled pitcher plant. If he had stayed one day longer, he never would have left alive.

"What's that, William?"

He waved the letter. "Nothing unusual, at least not now. Just a letter to a man who knew too much and died because of it." He stuffed the letter in his pocket. "I'll change into the suit upstairs and then we'll leave."

They stood for a moment on the doorsteps outside and Grossman said, "Why did the truck hit Professor Scott and not us, William?"

"Because whoever was driving it didn't have orders to, Karl. It wasn't Hart, he didn't even know we were there. While we were in the park, Hart was here, rifling the house." He started down the steps.

"Where are we going to stay tonight?"

Tanner frowned. "I don't know but I think it's a mistake to stay together all the time. If we do, it's putting all our eggs in one basket." He hesitated. "Tell you what—I'll meet you in the lobby of the Chicago public library tomorrow at ten, all right?"

Grossman nodded. "Be very careful, William."

"I've had a lot of experience along that line the last few days,

Karl. You just watch out for yourself." He walked down the street, turned the corner, and once more he was cut off and alone.

Nordlund.

Van Zandt.

DeFalco.

It was narrowing down fast, faster than Adam Hart could have figured on. Grossman had been eliminated, Scott had been killed, Petey had been identified as Hart's mistress. Marge could safely be counted out for obvious reasons.

Now there were only three.

Pick on any one, he thought, *and I'll be one-third right. Eeny, meeny, miny, mo, catch a superman by the toe. And if he hollers, don't let go. . . .*

Which left him with the problem of how he was going to get through the night. There was no sense in kidding himself. He had succeeded in distributing the danger between Grossman and himself but he was the case ace and Hart knew it.

It was getting towards dinnertime and the streets were emptying again. He caught the El back uptown and walked into one of the larger hotels in the Loop. He had cleaned up and had Scott's money; he was presentable, if not a fashion plate.

An events board in the lobby listed four different conventions going on in the hotel. He memorized the brief listing, then wandered into the bar. People, lots of people, for far into the night. Before the crowd started to thin, he would make contact and then he'd be good until morning again.

He juggled a small box in his pocket. Dextroamphetamine. Enough to keep him awake for a week. And after that?

But by then, of course, the game would be over—win, lose, or draw.

He picked a table in the corner where he could watch the people in the room and ordered beer. It was nearly eight o'clock and he was tracing wet rings on the marbelite top when he suddenly picked it up.

It was just an awareness, a feeling that somebody had come

into the room and quickly glanced over it. Somebody who had stopped for a moment a few tables away, looked at him, and then passed on.

He tensed, waiting for the prying and the probing but it never came. There was only a subtle aliveness to the air, a feeling of being watched. Whoever it was was still in the room, waiting for him to go to the john or do any one of a number of stupid things that would momentarily separate him from people.

He settled back in his chair and quietly inspected the room. It did no good. It was too smoky, there were too many pillars that people could hide behind, and it was doubtful if he could recognize anybody in the hazy atmosphere anyways. He turned back to the beer rings and pushed a finger around one of the circles, smearing the oval of dampness.

Somebody walked up to the table and sat down across from him.

"Bill."

He didn't look up. "You've got a chance to leave now, Marge. Stick around and you'll be tagged. Adam Hart's here."

"I don't know who you're talking about."

He kept his voice low and tried to hide his annoyance. "The mystery man, Marge. The man who moves little tents of paper on Saturday mornings just by looking at them. The man who murdered Olson. So be a nice girl and beat it."

"I'm not going to run out."

"It's not a question of personal bravery, it's just good common sense."

"I've been here too long already, then. It wouldn't make any difference now, would it?"

His voice became sarcastic. "It's really charitable of you to take such an interest in my welfare. You've really changed in two days. If I remember correctly, the last time I talked to you, you thought I was a murderer."

"It looked that way. Can you blame me?"

"Sure I can. You've known me long enough to know it couldn't be true."

"Maybe I made a mistake in coming over here."

"I've already told you that. Why don't you beat it?"

"You don't have to insult me to get me to leave."

"What *do* I have to do?"

"I don't have to take that," she said tightly. "From you or anybody else. So I thought it was possible you might have killed John. The police think so and they know more about that sort of thing than I do. Then I talked to Petey today and she doesn't even remember that she used to work for you!"

"And, clever girl that you are, you figured something was rotten in Denmark. Very bright."

She looked down at the table and didn't say anything.

"You haven't heard the rest of it," he said bitterly. "Professor Scott was killed today. And last night a little country doctor in South Dakota got his. I'll be suspect in both of those, too. What are you going to believe then?"

Her voice was low. "How many times do I have to say I'm sorry?"

He looked at her and tried to feel angry at the same time, then gave it up as a bad job.

"All right, so *I'm* sorry. I suppose I should have guessed it would end up this way." There was still the feeling of being watched, of having every little movement scrutinized. And there was the barest suggestion that the crowds would be clearing out shortly. Suddenly all the friendliness drained out of him. "How did you know I was here?"

"I didn't. I just came in here with my date—I think he's in the john right now. Very big fraternity man. I'll hold his hand on the way home and he'll tell all the boys at the house how he seduced me. You know the type."

He couldn't help smiling. "You better get back to that bar then before he comes out."

"Bill." She worried her lip between her teeth for a moment, then took the plunge. "I think you're going after this . . . Adam Hart. I think he might be a very dangerous man. And I can't help wondering if you shouldn't give it up."

"Who are you fronting for?"

She didn't slap his face, she didn't cry, she didn't get sore. "I'll make it very simple, Bill. I love you. I want to see you alive and not dead and if that sounds corny, I can't help it." She leaned towards him and he was suddenly very conscious of the smooth sweep of her breasts and the tan of her shoulders and the fine tone of her skin. The faint smell of her perfume and sweetly scented soap . . . "I'm lonely and I want you, which is something no girl is ever supposed to admit. But I'm tired of playing games and it doesn't look as if either one of us is going to have much time for them."

"I never got a proposal from a girl before."

"I'll bet this will be the only one, too."

He smiled. "It probably will be."

She stood up to go back to the bar. "Breakfast with me— pick me up say at nine tomorrow?"

"It's a date. In some nice, crowded restaurant." He watched her walk across the room, trying to catch a look at the guy she had gone out with. But people got in the way and her date kept his back turned and shortly afterwards, they left.

He went back to smearing his beer rings.

The feeling of tension was still in the room.

It was getting late and he was going to have to make contact soon. He stood up and sauntered over to the bar where a small group of men had been talking in loud whispers, then suddenly guffawing and slapping each other on the back. Name badges identified the group. He leaned casually on the bar and turned to face them. He glanced idly at one of the badges and his face lit up.

"Say, all you fellows in the kitchen-supply business?" They stopped talking and he knew he had sparked interest. "Got a brother in the business, runs the Amco supply house on the South Side."

"Y'don't say!"

A friendly clap on the shoulder.

"Hey, barkeep, bring a drink for m'friend here!"

A furious pumping of his hand.

"Didn't catch the name but mine's . . ."

"Amco, huh? Y'know, we've got a new line . . ."

"Little party going on upstairs . . ."

He was in.

There was no Amco and he had no brother but it wouldn't be difficult to string them for the evening. He could take his lead from what they had to say, maybe even accept verbal orders for his "brother." The party upstairs would be dull, of course. Cheap whiskey and tap water and "entertainers" supplied by the bell captain and too many people in too small a room.

But it would be a party that would keep going into the daylight hours, traveling from room to room. He couldn't have wanted anything better.

He drank with them in the bar and when they left and took the elevator up, he was still with them.

But so was the tension. It rode the elevator with him, a shadow he couldn't shake. The ghost that would sit in the corner and wait for him to make one small mistake. He turned, to try and locate it. . . .

"Face the front of the elevator, please."

The shadow went with him from party to party, always shifting or vanishing when he tried to pin it down. The rooms were filled with laughing, giggling, empty faces, trying to convince themselves and each other that they were having a great time. The loneliest faces in the world. And behind one of them . . . ?

But *which* one?

Early in the morning he suddenly discovered that he was slipping. He was drinking just a little too much, he was laughing just a little too hard, he was getting drunk a little too easy. Something was trying to push him along, like a butcher laying his thumb on the scale. Something was trying to add the straw to the camel's back.

Drinking and laughing and thinking it was so damned funny that they thought he had a brother who owned a warehouse. What a clever fellow he was, he ought to tell them the joke, just to see the look on their faces. They'd get a big bang out of it. . . .

A big bang . . .

He shook his head and tried to swim out of the alcoholic fog. Tell them what he had done, he thought thickly, and they'd throw him out. He'd be alone in the corridors and Hart would pounce on him before he could even get to the elevators.

He held a glass from then on but he didn't drink.

Five-thirty in the morning came very slowly and he could sense the tension being replaced by a feeling of disappointment. Sunrise and a faint, pink color behind the silhouetted skyline. Two more hours and there would be people on the streets and the city would be alive again.

He was suddenly sick to death of the smell of stale beer and the mumble of drunken conversation. There were about a dozen people in the party and they were nearly out on their feet. Glasses and empty bottles and small mountains of cigarette butts littered the room and in the corner somebody had been sick.

He sneered inwardly. The human race at its worst.

you agree . . .

It was just a drifting thought that plucked at his mind; he couldn't be sure but what he might have thought of it himself.

your pocket . . .

in your pocket . . .

look in your pocket . . .

He glanced quickly around. Nobody was looking at him, nobody was paying any attention to him. He walked over to the window and he could feel the skin crawl between his shoulder blades and knew that somebody in the room was watching him.

He put his hand in his pocket and felt a small piece of paper. Sometime during the evening he had been jostled and somebody had put it there. He took it out and unfolded it.

It read:

How do you like the zoo?

A neatly written signature that looked like copperplate:

Adam Hart.

Zoo? he thought.

The room and its impressions suddenly whirled around him, as hard and clear as cut glass.

A rock-and-roll tune blaring over the radio. A sudden suppressed giggle. The sound of liquid sloshing in a glass, a roar of animal laughter, the flushing of the water closet and water puddling in the sink, a woman's voice, "Now, *Charlie* . . .," somebody dropping a glass in the short hallway, the man on the bed waking up and vomiting over the side. . . .

And inside his mind, defeat and sudden twisting laughter before Adam Hart withdrew.

don't feed the animals . . .

14

IT was seven-thirty in the morning and a little too early for the Loop to fill with people on their way to work. Trucks were busy making deliveries before the Loop got crowded and the newspaper wagons were dropping off stacks of the *Tribune* and the *Times*. A few baggy-eyed businessmen were trotting out of the subway entrances but the Loop was still the private reservation of the newsstand vendors and the deliverymen. It would be another hour before the counter at Walgreen's became packed with secretaries drinking their breakfasts.

The sun was up and there wasn't a cloud in the sky. It was hot already and Tanner knew the day was going to be another scorcher.

He bought a paper and found himself an empty

booth in a drugstore. He ordered coffee and rolls for breakfast and took another dextroamphetamine capsule to keep himself going through the day. He took half an hour killing the coffee and rolls and another ten minutes glancing at the paper. A senator had died, a prominent actress had become involved in a New York vice trial, a government official had resigned over charges of corruption. And the police were still looking for a university professor who was wanted for questioning in a murder case. Oddly enough, the paper didn't run a mug shot of him. Thank God for small favors, he thought. It meant the police hadn't located a picture of him so neither the run-of-the-mill cop nor the general public could be expected to recognize him on sight.

He paid his bill and walked out to the now-crowded street.

Eight o'clock in the morning and he had nothing to do until he saw Marge for breakfast at nine. An hour to waste—and why not get to Marge's early? Spend some time talking about nothing at all, get his mind off his worries for once.

At least for thirty minutes.

He caught an El going north and was at her apartment by eight-twenty.

But there wasn't any Marge. He pressed the buzzer and could hear the faint ringing in the apartment but nobody came to answer the door. She might have gone out early, he thought, disappointed. And she might have forgotten about the breakfast date, which wasn't a pleasant thought but a possible one anyway.

He tried the knob from force of habit and the door swung quietly open. She must have forgotten to shut it all the way when she had left. Or else the lock had jammed and hadn't locked automatically when she closed the door; it happened sometimes. Or maybe . . . ?

Oh, God, no!

"Marge!" He raced in, glancing at the living room and throwing open the closet door. Then into the bedroom and the kitchen and a quick look into the bathroom. She wasn't there and he felt sick with relief, and then abruptly wondered just where she was. Stepped out just for a moment, probably. . . .

It was quiet and warm in the apartment, the sunlight strong and bright through the chintz-curtained windows. The room smelled sweet. The faint odor of "Tweed," he thought, Marge's trademark; what she called a "sensible" perfume. The apartment was a better setup than Petey's. A little larger, the carpeting not so worn, the wallpaper clean and modern.

That was what set it off. A modern room. A lot of light from the windows at the end, modernistic limed-oak furniture, wrought-iron lamps and chair frames, and a fish mobile over the desk, the fins moving slightly in a breeze from a half-open window. A large bed in the bedroom with a bookrack headboard and thick, round pillows. He ran his hand lightly over the coverlet, then turned it back and looked at the sheets. Good honest cotton.

He went back to the closet he had opened when he had first searched through for Marge. He hesitated, shrugged, and opened it up. Nothing but Marge's suits and dresses and he could identify almost every one. There were no hidden gowns, no fancy wraps.

The top of her dressing table was almost bare compared to Petey's. The large bottle of "Tweed" perfume, powder, rouge, and lipsticks. A small box for hairpins and curlers. A large picture frame standing on top of the dresser, with no photograph in it. Probably a new frame she hadn't had time to fit a photo for.

He started for the door, thinking of waiting outside in the hallway, then paused halfway across the room, feeling vaguely unhappy about something. A nice, modern room, he thought. Neat, airy, attractive. But almost like a room in a hospital. It was designed not to be lived in but to suit somebody's esthetic taste. And not Marge's. Marge had always struck him as the type who would have her laundry in the bathroom sink, stockings drying on a towel on the radiator, and bobby pins scattered loose over the dressing table top.

But there was something more specific, something that had struck him as a clue. . . .

He slowly walked back to the center of the room, searching

for the something that hadn't fitted, the something that had stuck out like the proverbial sore thumb. Not the mobile, not the clothes in the closet, not the dressing table.

The dresser.

The large frame on top of it that had no picture in it.

People bought frames because they had pictures to go in them, he thought slowly. They didn't buy the frames first and wait for the pictures to come later. At least, most people didn't. And Marge had had a photograph to put in that frame, one he had given her the previous Christmas. One of himself.

He took the frame down and looked at it closely. It wasn't a new frame, there was a little tarnish around the edges. And there was a sheet of photo paper in it. A sheet of plain, white photo paper but with no picture on it.

But Marge saw something when she looked at it, he thought. She saw a picture there.

Adam Hart's.

Marge had been the Judas goat. Sure, have breakfast with her at nine—but she had never meant to be there. Somebody else would have been waiting for him. He would have had breakfast with Adam Hart instead, and that would have been the last breakfast he would ever have had.

The night before, when he had been in the car, he thought suddenly. How odd that of all the hotels in the Loop, he and Marge should have hit the same one. And her date, the escort he had never quite seen. The tension had dropped off for a few minutes after Marge had left, and then it had come back—strong.

Adam Hart had taken her home and then returned.

And Tanner had believed everything that Marge had told him.

The clock on the dresser chimed once. Eight-thirty. Time to get the hell out of there.

He looked down at the frame he held, then broke it over his knee, shattering the glass and cutting his hand. He didn't give a damn.

He walked out and slammed the door behind him.

* * *

Grossman was waiting for him at the library, nervously pacing back and forth in front of the information booth. He was making himself too obvious, Tanner thought. He should have been in the reading room, supposedly absorbed in a newspaper or book.

The physicist saw him and hurried over. "What are we going to do today, William?"

"Go right ahead with what we intended to do. Eliminate another committee member, somebody who might be useful to us."

Grossman wet his lips. "Which one? Professor Van Zandt? DeFalco?"

"Neither. I was thinking of Arthur Nordlund."

"Why him?"

"Why not? He's a young man, a strong man. And one who has contacts that might do us some good—if he's the McCoy and if we can convince him."

Grossman nodded. "All right. Then we shall lay a trap for Commander Nordlund."

Tanner looked around and spotted a pay phone in the hall just a short distance from the reading room. He took down the phone number. "I'll be gone for a while, Karl. I'll call you back here."

He left the library and turned south on State Street. There was a little print shop just south of the Loop that he had discovered when he had once audited an undergraduate criminology course. A shop that could fix him up with some kind of identification before he started looking into the background of Arthur Nordlund.

He ticked off on his fingers what he knew about the man. Early thirties, though like most predominately thin men, he didn't look that old. Hardly an athlete but not exactly soft either; a "stringy" build. An unfriendly personality that annoyed most people; he wasn't pleasant to talk to, he wasn't pleasant to be with. People would steer away from him. If he died tomorrow, it wouldn't take long for most people to forget him.

He stopped in a drugstore and thumbed through the phone book, then made a brief call, disguising his voice. Commander Nordlund wasn't expected in until late afternoon, if then. Which meant there would be a clear field with the personnel in Nordlund's office.

There were other Navy officers in the building on Rush Street. Nordlund's was at the end of the hallway, an unpretentious cubbyhole manned by a cute Wave and a plump first-class yeoman who was leaning comfortably back in his swivel chair, half asleep.

He snapped wide awake when Tanner opened the door. "Yes, sir?"

"Commander Nordlund in?"

He wasn't. The desk at the rear of the room even looked like it had dust on it. But the tone of Tanner's voice let the yeoman know he hadn't expected to find Nordlund in and, in fact, hadn't wanted to. The official stamp.

"No, sir. He probably won't be here until afternoon— maybe not even then. Something I can do?"

Tanner nodded towards the girl who had paused in her typing and was watching them. "I'd like to talk to you alone."

The yeoman fished a coin out of his watch pocket and flipped it to the girl. "Coffee, Sue. Cream and no sugar and don't hurry back." After she had gone, he asked: "What's the pitch?"

Tanner took the forged card out of his wallet and let it drop on the desk. "Naval Intelligence. Commander Haskell downstairs said I should talk to you. About the Commander." He had picked Haskell's name off the directory in the lobby.

The yeoman moistened thick lips and Tanner could see him flipping through a mental card file of everything he knew about Nordlund, looking for anything that might be incriminating to himself.

"Anything I can do to help, just ask me, sir. The Commander's a fine man, sir, one of the finest officers I ever met in the Navy. I . . ."

Tanner cut him off. "Maybe it would be better if I asked the questions. I don't think it will take so long that way."

The yeoman froze in mid-sentence. "Yes, sir."

"You've known Commander Nordlund for a long time?"

"Yes, sir. We were stationed on the same destroyer during the Gulf War."

Tanner sat down in the chair the Wave had vacated and leaned comfortably back. "He had a pretty good record, didn't he? We've got his service file, of course, but I mean unofficially."

"He had a fine record, sir. And I never saw him get shook once. Cool head, never got rattled. Good mind for decisions."

"Any unusual political views?" He could tell by the yeoman's expression that the sailor thought this was the clutch question.

"I don't remember him having any political views at all, sir."

"Any hobbies, did he play cards much, gamble?"

"I don't remember, sir."

"You said you knew him pretty well."

"That was a while back, sir."

"This is just routine check," Tanner said carefully. "We're not trying to get something on the Commander and so far as we know, he hasn't done anything wrong."

Some of the careful reserve vanished. "He gambled a little. Not much, but a little."

"How is he with the women?"

"He doesn't get around much, sir. He's not the type. Oh, he has his girl friends but he isn't the ladykiller kind, if you follow me."

"I follow you. You don't know if he's ever dated a girl named Patricia Olson, do you?" He pretended to consult a folded sheet of paper he took out of his pocket. "She's the secretary for the human research project over at the university."

A fleeting look of surprise. "Hell no, sir. I've seen her around—he's got better taste than that."

Tanner leaned forward and smiled confidentially. "Just between you and me, what do you think of the Commander?"

The yeoman didn't take the bait. "I think he's an excellent officer, sir. Maybe not the friendliest in the world but he knows what he's doing and that's more than you can say for some of them."

Which about wound it up except for one small point. Something he had remembered from his trip to Brockton and that he had seen an example of in Marge's apartment.

"You don't have a recent photograph of the Commander around the office, do you? I remember seeing him once several years ago and of course we have photos in the files, but they're not recent."

"I'm sorry, sir, but I can't remember his ever having one around. We could have one made up if you wanted it. . . ."

Tanner stood up. "That's all right. Incidentally, I'd appreciate it if you wouldn't tell the Commander I was here. We're not through yet and we want an unbiased check."

"I understand, sir."

Tanner was almost out the door when the yeoman said, "Say, wait a minute!" He waddled over to a filing cabinet and pawed among the papers for a moment. He finally came back with a form with a small photograph attached to the upper right-hand corner. "The Commander filled out this form and was going to send it in to Bupers about six months ago but the form's obsolete now. Maybe this photo would help."

Tanner glanced at it. "No, I don't think so. It's a little small for what I would like."

The photograph was blurred and fuzzy, it could have been a picture of any Navy officer.

Which meant that Arthur Nordlund had suddenly been promoted to a red-hot prospect. . . .

Smile at the Wave at the information desk on your way out. Find out from her that the Commander almost always gets in late, that he lives in an apartment hotel just off Diversey Parkway and takes his breakfast in a little coffee shop just around the corner.

And don't embarrass her about how she knows all this. The Com-

mander is no lady-killer but it's only natural that a pretty Wave who works in the same building should know him rather well. . . .

Take the El north and stroll past the coffee shop and casually glance in. The Commander is sitting at a table in the rear, toying with grapefruit and burnt toast. His face is just a shade worn this morning, the faint traces of fatigue beneath his eyes.

Just a healthy good time the night before?

Or did he ever go to bed at all? Did he spend the evening in a hotel room at a cheap convention party watching a harried anthropology professor trying to keep alive during the long night?

Possibly, but don't think about it and don't watch too long. A quick look and keep on walking so he can't pick up your thoughts. It wouldn't pay to tip your hand now.

And then there's the possibility that you're mistaken and Adam Hart is actually watching you watching Nordlund and laughing to beat the band. This is a watchbird watching you. . . .

Buy the paper on the corner and have a Coke in the drugstore kitty-corner from the coffee shop. You finish it in a hurry when Nordlund suddenly gets up and pays his bill and strolls outside. You're at the cash register when you see him flag a cab and you don't even wait for your change. There's another taxi outside and you catch that and tell the driver to follow Nordlund's cab. It's hard to tell when you're being tailed down Michigan Boulevard. There are so many cars. And besides, Nordlund isn't expecting this and won't be looking for it.

Or will he?

Nordlund's cab stopped at the athletic club. Tanner drove up a block and got out, swearing to himself. The club was for members only; he couldn't get in. And there was no telling how long Nordlund would be there.

He walked across the Drive to a park bench on the lake front and sat down and unfolded his paper. No matter how long the Commander stayed, he was going to wait him out.

He had been waiting a bare half hour before the Navy man came out, dressed in white ducks and T shirt and with a rolled-up towel under his arm. Probably going swimming at a nearby beach . . .

On the sidewalk, Nordlund lit a cigarette and leaned against the building, watching the passers-by. Tanner hid behind the paper. Nordlund was waiting for somebody. . . .

Two cigarettes later, a girl in tennis shorts ran up to Nordlund, kissed him lightly on the cheek, and they stood on the walk and talked for a while. *The date,* Tanner thought. While he was watching, the girl suddenly frowned and pointed to Nordlund's towel. The Commander snapped his fingers and made a face, then gestured down the street towards the beach. The girl started walking, turned, waved once, and went on.

Nordlund walked to the street and hailed a cab. Tanner caught one right behind him and trailed him back to his apartment on Diversey Parkway. He parked while Nordlund ran into the building.

The girl had gone on ahead, he thought, while Nordlund had driven back to the apartment. Why? Because he had forgotten something? Maybe a blanket, maybe a portable radio?

The cab driver drummed his fingers against the steering wheel. "Why so interested in him, Mac? You got somethin' on him?"

"Let's just say he owes me money."

The driver nodded wisely. "One of those guys, huh? Y'know, they're all alike—live in fancy apartments and owe everybody in town."

The minutes limped slowly by. *What the hell could be keeping him?* Tanner thought. *A dash in, a minute to get whatever he had forgotten, and a quick dash out.*

Five minutes.

Ten minutes.

A half hour.

The mailman made his rounds down the street and walked into the apartments and talked to the girl at the switchboard; Tanner could just get a glimpse of her through the big glass doors. An old man in a Western Union uniform tottered in and three girls, probably secretaries, came out. A laundry truck drove up and a binful of white linen disappeared through the doors. A couple of kids wandered by, tossing a ball back and forth among themselves.

The cab that Nordlund had come in suddenly clashed gears and moved up the street.

Tanner's own driver stirred restlessly. "Doesn't look like he's coming out. I think he's given you the slip."

"Wait a few minutes longer."

The driver shook his head. "Uh-uh. This is a busy time of day and I'm losin' a lot of fares as is. I'm gonna have to beat it."

Tanner paid him off, then walked into the drugstore on the corner where he could watch the entrance of the apartment building. He leafed through the magazines at the newsstand and had himself a cup of coffee.

Forty minutes.

He walked over to the phone booth, left the door halfway open so he could still see the apartments, and called Grossman. He could go up alone but there was no sense in taking chances that he didn't have to.

One hour. Grossman drove up in a cab and barged into the drugstore, his fat face sweaty. "He has not come out yet?"

"Not yet—and it shouldn't have taken him longer than a few minutes. Let's go up."

At the desk, the woman said, "Commander Nordlund has apartment 607. I'll give him a ring." Before he could stop her she was buzzing the room. There was no answer. She frowned. "Now that's odd. He *should* be in. He had a visitor just a little while ago. . . ."

The noises from the street were suddenly very sharp.

"What visitor?"

She looked flustered. "Why, a gentleman who came in a little over half an hour ago—I think that was about the time. Is something wrong? What on earth's the matter?"

"What did he look like?"

"Well, I should say he was a very distinguished-looking gentleman." Her face softened a little. "Really, a very fine appearance and very dignified. Tall and somewhat thin, steel-gray hair, a small salt-and-pepper moustache . . ."

There was the same subtle change in her voice and the same distant look in her eyes, Tanner thought. He had seen the same look and heard the same sort of tremolo when he had been in Brockton. From the little girl who had served him breakfast at the hotel.

"I think," he said gently, "that all of us should go up. I don't think the Commander is feeling very well."

"*Oh!*" She told the other girl at the switchboard to take over and scurried out from behind the counter. About fifty, Tanner thought, and a little on the dumpy side. Like the girl in Brockton, she had seen the man she had wanted to see. She caught the burly laundryman just as he was leaving. "Jeff, help us a minute, will you? A man on the sixth floor is ill!"

Now there were four of them, Tanner thought. Maybe enough to handle Adam Hart if he had stayed behind. . . .

The floors slipped by in silence and he could feel the jitters begin. What if Hart was still there? So there were four of them, but that was no guarantee. It would take sudden surprise and shock and no thought at all about what he was going to do. He took the Beretta from his pocket and checked it. The woman's eyes widened and the laundryman looked surprised and said, "What's the idea, mister?"

He didn't answer and when the elevator doors slid back, he hit the corridor, running. 601—603—605 . . .

He crashed into the door with his shoulder. It hadn't been locked, it hadn't even been closed tightly, and he stumbled halfway through the living room before he could stop himself.

It took him a full ten seconds to realize that there was nobody there, that there was no tension and there wasn't going to be any plucking at his mind. But there was a subtle electricity to the air, as faint as a woman's perfume, and he got the impression that somebody *had* been there and just a moment before.

And then Grossman was shouting from the bedroom, "In here! Come quickly!"

15

NORDLUND'S eyes were half closed, the muscles in his face rigid and his loose linen shirt soaked with sweat. He had sagged to his knees by the bed, one hand clutching at the spread. He was suffering from primary shock, Tanner thought. The skin was cold, the pulse so feeble as to be almost undetectable, the breathing shallow.

"Nordlund!"

He got his hands under the man's armpits and lifted him onto the bed. The laundryman and the woman who had been at the desk downstairs were staring. She started to edge towards the door. "Maybe I better call a doctor. . . ."

He was panicky for a moment, then flipped open his wallet and showed her the faked identity card for Naval

Intelligence. "I'd appreciate it if you wouldn't. But you might go downstairs and get some hot coffee." He jerked a thumb at the laundryman who was looking helpless. "You, help me get him undressed and under the covers—he'll come around in a few minutes." He loosened the laces in Nordlund's shoes and a moment later they had him under the blankets. Warmth and hot drink and Nordlund would recover all right. But it was a wonder the man was still alive.

"What d'ya think did him in? Somebody get in or something?"

Tanner was blunt. "Don't you have laundry to deliver, jocko?"

"Yeah, sure, I guess I do." The laundryman turned in the doorway. "Next time you want help," he said bitterly, "ask somebody else."

I'm still a flub at human relations, Tanner thought. *But damnit, I couldn't have let him stay. . . .*

"Watch the Commander, will you, Karl?"

He walked back to the living room and looked around. The table by the window, a chair moved slightly away from it as if somebody had been sitting there. Nordlund had walked in and was probably in the bedroom when Hart had come up and sat down. Towards the bedroom itself, a chair had been overturned and a lamp shattered on the floor.

So Nordlund had come out and tried to fight and they had gone to it for a few minutes, he thought. And Nordlund had been partially successful; at least he had lived long enough so that help could arrive. The sheerest sort of luck, the one chance in a million that depended on somebody's watching him and finally getting curious as to why he hadn't come back down from his apartment.

Tanner walked back to the bedroom and looked at Nordlund with a good deal more respect. Nordlund was about his own height and thin, maybe about a hundred and fifty pounds, with thin wrists and slight shoulders and a narrow chest. But in other respects he must have been a bear of a man.

The coffee came up and he tried to pour some into the slack

mouth. It didn't work very well; a little dribbled in but a lot more slopped over on the sheets. He pressed the jaws open, held down the tongue with a finger, and tried again. It worked a little better but it was still a messy proposition.

Grossman had shown the woman out and come back. "Should we call a doctor, William? He does not look good."

"No, he'll be all right." He took his pipe from his pocket and noticed for the first time that his own hands were shaking. "It was a close call."

"I would not want to come closer."

"Do you think he was working on a separate line of investigation? After all, you were, Scott was, and I was."

"Perhaps, although he did not seem inclined to believe what happened that Saturday morning."

Tanner stood up. "Let's take a look around."

They turned the apartment upside down. There was nothing, outside of personnel work that Nordlund had been doing for the Navy. A sheaf of carbons of transcripts of the meetings at the university, some personnel records, and a large file of restricted naval publications.

There was a small noise from the bedroom and Tanner raced back. Nordlund was sitting up, his eyes staring.

"It's all right, Commander, he's gone. You're going to be all right."

The light in Nordlund's eyes faded and he sagged back on the pillow. *"Oh, God!"*

Tanner waited a moment for Nordlund to recover and then asked the question he had been wanting to ask for the last hour. "Who was he, Commander?"

Nordlund shook his head. "I never managed to see his face, Tanner. He walked in and then we were at it. I never saw his face, he never let me see it! *Do you know what it's like, Tanner, for a man to slip into your mind and start driving you like he would drive a car?"*

His voice started to shake and Tanner said, "Take it easy. Hart isn't here and he's not coming back, at least for a while. And I know what it feels like, I've been through it, too."

The horror of it suddenly washed back on Nordlund and he shook underneath the covers; he bit his own wrist to keep from screaming. Tanner watched him curiously and waited for the spasm of fear to go away. Nordlund's eyes were red-rimmed and sunken, his face a fine grid of jumping muscles. His nerves were shot, Tanner thought. Somebody had taken the starch out of the man, somebody had snipped the wires that had strung him together.

He said, "What have you done since that Saturday morning, Commander?"

"What do you mean?"

"Did you try investigating Olson or any others on the committee, anything like that?"

"No, I didn't think it was necessary." Nordlund's mouth tightened. "I saw everything that you people saw but it didn't make sense to me. I thought that perhaps a draft had moved the paper—you thought that yourself at the time."

Poor, pragmatic little Navy man, Tanner thought. He believed what he could touch and nothing else, and after Saturday he had been in over his depth and floundering around. He hadn't known what to believe.

"And after Olson was killed?"

Nordlund looked away. "They said you did that. I believed them. And you had disappeared, it seemed logical."

"And Professor Scott?"

"Old men are killed crossing the street every day." His voice turned bitter. "I was pretty stupid, wasn't I?"

"You were, but that's water over the dam. Maybe I ought to bring you up to date."

After he had finished, Nordlund said, "It's easier to believe in the Abominable Snowman."

"Do you think I'm lying, Commander?"

Nordlund shivered. "God, no. If I was any firmer a believer, I'd be dead."

Tanner walked to the window. It was getting late. A few more hours and night would have rolled over the city. And the problem of what to do when the sun went down would be with him. "There's three of us now and we've got two men to go after. Who will be first, Van Zandt or DeFalco?"

Nordlund closed his eyes. "You make the decision, Professor. I don't know enough about either one of them."

"There is not a great deal to know," Grossman said precisely. "Van Zandt was born in Belgium—1950, I believe. His father was a baker, his mother was a seamstress. He came to this country at the age of ten. A precocious child, from what other faculty members have told me. He did his undergraduate work at Beloit and his graduate work at Harvard. A brilliant student. Professionally, he has written a number of papers on the psychology of factory workers—invaluable, I understand, if you are interested in that sort of thing."

"What about DeFalco?"

"I do not know much about him. He was born in 1967, here in Chicago. An above-average student, though not exceptionally so, and very much the athlete. He was expelled from school during his senior year and readmitted after a month. He has done both his undergraduate and graduate work here."

"All that's from the records," Tanner said. "Which means that only one of those backgrounds is true."

Which left them about where they had started, he thought. *Power, power, who has the Power?*

Professor Harold Van Zandt—cold, distant, bitter? Or Edward DeFalco, the DeFalco who had been so scared that morning in the cemetery. Or had that been an act, too?

"Any suggestions?"

Nordlund's thin hands plucked at the blankets. His voice was so low Tanner almost didn't hear him. "We could go away—we could run. Hide where he could never find any of us."

"And spend the rest of our lives wondering if we were safe? You don't think Adam Hart's going to forget you, do you, Commander?"

Nordlund sighed. "All right, so I was just making noises."

"Karl?"

"I think, perhaps, we ought to eliminate DeFalco first. There is probably less chance of him actually being *it* and then that would make four of us on our side."

Nordlund struggled up in bed. There was a little color in his cheeks and his eyes didn't look quite as whipped as they had. "Aren't we beating around the bush? We've got it down to two, why take chances?"

It took Tanner a moment to catch on.

"Well, what's wrong with it?" Nordlund asked sharply. "If you were in a war you wouldn't hesitate. The longer we wait, the less chance we have. Why take the risk?"

"I would not want to kill a man in cold blood," Grossman whispered, "without knowing for sure."

The idea couldn't be so easily dismissed, Tanner thought. But to identify Hart and to kill him were two entirely different things. Murdering Van Zandt and DeFalco was possible, a sniper's bullet would do it. But if the first shot missed, they'd never get another chance. And to kill a man who might be innocent . . . He said, "Would you have seen anything wrong with it when there were three of you to eliminate?"

"It wouldn't have made any difference," Nordlund said, but he didn't sound convinced.

"Do you think you can get out of bed?"

Nordlund tried it. "I'm a little weak but outside of that, I guess I'm all right. What do we do now?"

"The first thing to do is to get out of here. Just because Hart failed the first time doesn't mean he's going to leave you alone. The police will probably be coming around a few minutes from now—they'll have some charge worked out." He felt a brief surge of sympathy for Nordlund. "You realize you're all washed up in the Navy, don't you, Commander? Your records will disappear and somebody will dream up some reason to nail you."

"I've thought about that." Nordlund went to the clothes closet and started packing a small overnight case. "What do we do the rest of the evening?"

"That's up to you. We'll split up for the night and meet tomorrow morning, say the same place I met Karl this morning. Ten o'clock in the lobby of the public library downtown."

They took the elevator down and separated on the sidewalk outside. Nordlund started north. Grossman bought a paper at the newsstand and turned west. Tanner watched them go and started back to the Loop.

It was suppertime and the walks were crowded with people hurrying home. A few more hours and the sun would be down and another long night would have begun.

How many nights had he hidden? he wondered.

How many nights had he spent hiding behind closed doors and drawn shades, waiting for Adam Hart to show up in person? And how many nights had he walked the streets trying to stay with the crowds or spent the night with a drunken party, anything to keep from being alone?

He was walking through the Loop again. Maybe he could hit another hotel and invite himself into another convention party. . . .

But it wouldn't be easy to stay awake all night again. He already felt half dead with fatigue. The dextroamphetamine was losing its effect and he felt jumpy, skittery. Nerves. His were only going to take so much. And once he was off the dextro binge and had fallen asleep?

He laughed to himself. It wouldn't take much to kill him then. A child with a blunt instrument could do it.

He yawned and shook his head and forced himself to take an interest in the city and the people around him. *Funny,* he thought, *I've forgotten how ugly the city can look. At night it's all neon and chrome and plastic but you can look above the level of the lights and see the old buildings through the glitter.*

The buildings, all angles and ugly corners and covered with soot and grime and pigeon shit. The bright, flashy store fronts, glass and chrome and stainless steel, and above them the sordid, cluttered architecture of the early 1900s. The dirty, littered lanes of tar that passed for streets and the flashing, raucous signs. The ugly street lamps and the squat metal boxes that said *Keep Our City Clean.* The imitation Roman of the Art Institute and the hideous building that was the public library and the modernistic messes that were the cheap jewelry stores and the cut-rate clothing shops.

And the people.

The jostling, greedy, overdressed, stupid people. The fat man in the restaurant window, drowning himself in a bowl of spaghetti; the overdressed woman window shopper, her face cast in a mold of powder and rouge, dreaming of buying more clothes than she could ever possibly wear; the teen-ager, thick black hair waved out over his temples and his sport coat drooping over narrow shoulders, staring at a nude dummy in another window.

Every little imperfection magnified a hundred-fold. Every little fault exaggerated out of all proportion.

Hart! he thought.

Somewhere in the crowds behind him, giving him the special guided tour of the city. Somehow he would have to shake him. . . .

He stopped and looked at the display in an out-of-season fruit store and tried to blot Hart out of his mind. The apples in the window weighed a pound a piece and the grapefruit were as big as a boy's head and the plums looked as large as oranges. A clerk was lettering a sign on the inside of the glass with white wash. The sign read:

Had enough?

He blinked and turned away. An empty alley where the delivery trucks could come up to the service entrances. A quick dodge down it and maybe into the store's rear entrance . . .

He was two steps into the alley when he suddenly caught the absence of any pressure on him, the watchful waiting. The *expectant* waiting. Up the alley and he would be all alone. Death would be waiting for him at the end of it. Sudden and quick this time and just as final as John Olson's had been.

He turned away from the alley and it was like walking in

glue. Hart had insinuated himself into partial control. He staggered and people on the sidewalk stared at him, their faces carefully blank or curious or filled with disgust. Then he was back on the walk and the contact was broken.

Somewhere, a mental shrug.

I'll have to watch it. People will stare and then some old biddy will say, "Mr. Policeman, look at that man! Isn't that terrible?" And then a cop will run me in and five will get you ten that this time I won't be lucky.

He walked past a novelty shop where a man was printing up headlines on phony front pages. A pause to watch the man take the paper off the bed of type and paste it in the window.

It was a two-line banner.

IT'S A LOUSY WORLD
ISN'T IT, TANNER?

A lousy world. Adam Hart's world would be so much neater, so much better organized, people would be so much happier. . . .

He had to get away!

He ran across State Street on the tag end of a green light, cutting off most of the crowd behind him. Into the corner Walgreen's and past the lunch counter. Something tugged at his mind and he glanced at the menu a high-school girl was holding. There were the usual late-evening specials listed and a small piece of white paper clipped to the top.

Feed the animals?

He circled through the drugstore, then out again and into a subway entrance. He didn't go down to the train platforms but crossed through the passage over to the branch that ran beneath Dearborn Street. The sound of his heels echoed through the tile-lined passage and there was a tentative groping in the air behind him.

Then he ran up the exit stairs and was seeing the city as he had always seen it. The solidity and majesty of the Board of Trade building, the simple, marble beauty of St. Peter's, the sharp lines of the Prudential building. And the people on the walks, some handsome, some homely, some marked with the signs of easy or hard living. Not all good, not all bad. Just people—for whom he suddenly felt a vast affection.

It hit him then and he almost went under. A sudden clutching at his mind, the familiar, heavy squeezing; but this time an attack designed to overwhelm him quickly.

He stumbled and leaned against the building for support, momentarily closing his eyes. The pressure dropped a little but it was still there, still grinding down on him, and he knew he couldn't resist it for more than a few minutes. He had never thought that Hart would attempt control in public, that he would run the risk of giving himself away. But neither had he considered what Hart would do if he were desperate.

He glanced wildly up the street. People on the walks, but no police car. Cars parked by the curb. And one that had just shouldered its way into a parking spot, the owner getting out and still holding the keys in his hand. Tanner ran up to him and tore the keys away and slid into the car. He slammed the door in the man's face and locked it, then savagely thumbed the starter.

"Police! Where's the cops? Goddamnit, he's stealing my car!"

People started to run up the walk and boil out of the all-night restaurants, some of them still clutching sandwiches. The owner started to beat at the door.

He hit the starter again and the motor came alive with a roar. He pulled away from the curb, scraping the fender of the car in front of him. The man who had been pounding at the door fell away from the side.

Speed, he thought blindly. Speed to get out of there while he was still breathing, while his heart still pumped. And distance to separate him from Adam Hart. . . .

Already Hart's control was slipping. He could feel himself start to breathe more normally, his heart to slow down to an average beat. He roared down Randolph, running the stop lights, and then he was out of the Loop. Far behind him he could hear the shriek of sirens.

He was still running risks, he thought. But if he had to take a chance, he would rather take it this way.

Then he caught a glimpse in the rear-view mirror. There was another car on the silvered pavement, running without lights, turning whenever he turned. He floored the gas pedal but the car behind him still clung.

Randolph and Ogden and then he was skidding through the light night traffic onto Washington Boulevard. On Washington he could feel the feeble pluckings at his mind again. Minute stirrings and shivers and then another sudden attempt at full control.

His hands froze on the wheel and he nearly drove over the curb and into the street lamps.

Somewhere, silent laughter.

Faster! Oh, my God, faster!

The night reeled by outside the car windows. The apartment buildings and the shuttered houses and the haloed street lamps.

Winking out, one by one.

He shook his head and opened his eyes wide. The lights were growing dimmer. Hart was narrowing his attempts at control, limiting it to just the eyes. The world was fading, the moon and the stars were blinking out and the lighted houses were shadows that flickered by like gray ghosts. A few minutes more and he would be driving blind, trying to thread his way out of the city in pitch blackness.

Then he had a sudden urge to turn the car and drive north. An imperative, demanding urge.

Why?

He froze to the wheel and kept straight on, the street and the city a darkening, pitch-black mist. And then, very faintly, he caught it. The faraway plaintive bellowing of a train whistle. Somewhere ahead was a train crossing, the red light winking and the wooden arms down and the alarm clanging away.

He caught himself swerving at the intersections as something tried to force him into the side streets, away from the
crossing far ahead.

Then he was driving in pure blackness, the bellowing of the
train whistle hammering his ears. A jar and a splintering noise
and the sound of his tires thrumming across the rails. Then the
bellowing was behind him and drawing away. He kept the gas
pedal to the floor and prayed.

The yellow street lamps flared briefly like candles that had
just been lit, guttered for a second, then swiftly grew to brilliant
luminescence. The stars flickered into view and the houses
along the Boulevard settled back into sight like objects at the
bottom of a muddy but clearing stream.

The freight was a long one, it was going to hold up traffic
for minutes. He was blocks away from Hart now and he knew
that he was free for the rest of the evening. There were still
problems, of course. There were the police, who would be
looking for a stolen car. Which meant that he would have to
ditch it, and soon.

And there was the minor question of where he was going to
spend the night.

16

HE abandoned the car near the city limits and then walked long blocks back to a park that was comfortably crowded with people sleeping out in the open. There would be bugs and he'd get grass stains and the air was still enough so he would hear every little whisper. But it was safer than a hotel room and not as stuffy and the air didn't smell of cheap disinfectant.

He walked through the lanes of the park and paused at the other side. Beyond was a strip of clay, strewn with tin cans and crumpled cardboard boxes, bordering a drainage canal. There was a sharp slope and then a narrow, grassy ledge just above the surface of the water. Shadowed and safer, perhaps, than the park itself.

He slid quietly down the slope and lay down on the

dried grass. He stared at the moon and the stars overhead and then dozed off and slept fitfully until dawn.

He woke up with the birds, in the early morning when the sky is a candy pink. He yawned and got to his feet and walked through the park until he came out on a business street. He was still miles away from the Loop and the ten-o'clock rendezvous with Grossman.

Early on a Thursday morning.

How much longer can I last?

He glanced at two factory workers boarding a bus and felt in his pocket for money. A few coins, but not enough.

He shrugged and started walking.

It was a warm morning and he walked slowly and watched the city wake up. People in the parks and on the fire escapes, stretching in the early morning sunlight and hawking and spitting and scratching themselves. The women in dirty bathrobes, their hair in curlers and their tired faces sagging at the edges. Fat men in pajamas too small for them and skinny men in shorts and T shirts looking at the world as if it were a suit they had bought at a second floor walk-up and they were just getting a good look at it in the daylight.

The homely little people who made up ninety-nine per cent of the world, who made all the mistakes and committed all the crimes and regretted everything they had ever done which had given them a little pleasure in life. The decent little people who were kind to strangers and deprived themselves of necessities so their kids could have the luxuries and who got their heads shot off in the once-every-generation war. The poor slobs who lived in ratty little apartments that smelled of stale cooking and human sweat or were making payments on cheesebox homes with sprung door-frames and commodes you could hear all over the house whenever somebody flushed them.

Most of them were neither sinners nor saints but a fine combination of both—carefully mixed and blended so only the most expensive psychiatrists could ever untangle them. There were the few who would plant grass and flowers in their back yards year after year even though they knew flowers would never grow on a diet of broken glass and city soot, there were the few who would become interested in the arts without becoming phonies, and there were always the kids who could be enthusiastic about life despite being raised in garbage cans.

They were the few who stood to lose the most if Adam Hart were running things. Most people would be perfectly willing to turn the world over to Hart and say, "Here, you run it for a while."

But how the hell could he be so sure that Hart wanted it?

It was ten o'clock when he made the Loop and walked into the library. Grossman and Nordlund weren't there.

They weren't there at eleven.

They weren't there at noon.

At one o'clock Nordlund walked in. It took Tanner a minute to recognize him. The white ducks and the linen shirt had disappeared. The moccasins had been replaced by black shoes and he was wearing a lightweight blue-serge suit that made him look five years older. He had dyed his hair brown and maybe it was only the lighting but the lines in his face looked deeper.

"I stole the suit," Nordlund said dryly. "It's the first thing I ever stole."

"It won't be the last. Where did you stay last night?"

"In a car—the kind where the front seat folds down to make a bed."

Nordlund was resourceful, Tanner thought. He was going to be handy to have around.

Nordlund suddenly realized that Grossman wasn't there. "Where's Karl?"

"I was hoping that he'd be with you."

The Navy man looked concerned. "I haven't seen him since we separated last night."

Scratch another one, Tanner thought grimly. Karl wouldn't have been late, something must have happened to him. To the best of his knowledge, the police hadn't been looking for him, which left—Adam Hart.

"What do we do now, Professor?" Nordlund asked expectantly.

Tanner felt tired. His muscles ached from lying on the ground, and he had slept all night in his clothes and knew he smelled. He wanted a shave and a shower and he wanted to sleep between clean sheets for once—sleep soundly without worrying about the night's sleep being his last. And he was tired of playing George and having everybody else let *him* do it. Quite a few other people had a stake in what was happening, too.

"How good are you at playing Sherlock, Commander?"

"Detective? I could give it a try."

To Nordlund, Tanner thought, life had probably been one old college try after another and it had always paid off for him. He wondered if the man actually knew what he was up against. Then he was annoyed with himself for getting annoyed. At least Nordlund was resilient, he hadn't been beaten down.

But then, he hadn't been running for two weeks, either.

"There are only two committee members left, Commander. One of them is it. We don't know much about either one, particularly what they've been doing these last two weeks. I think we ought to find out. You take DeFalco, I'll take Van Zandt. Find out as much as you can about what he's been doing and we'll meet out in front tonight—say about eleven." He hesitated. "Be careful—you'll be doing good if you can just stay alive that long."

After Nordlund had left, Tanner went to the newsstand outside and bought all the early editions of the afternoon papers. He took them back to the library reading room and spread them out on one of the tables. If something had happened to Grossman, there was an off chance the papers would have a story on it.

They didn't, but two other stories caught his eye. One was a page one story on himself—the usual killer-at-large stuff—with detailed descriptions of the murder and a two-column cut of John Olson. It was old news but it was being played up big. There was no photograph of himself.

The other story was a science feature about the Man of To-morrow. It was well done and scientifically accurate. But then, he thought, it should have been.

It was written by Professor Harold Van Zandt.

He had a long time to kill before nightfall, he thought. He could spend some time trying to find out what had happened to Grossman but he had a hunch he wouldn't have much success. It would be more profitable to check up on one Harold Van Zandt, jealous colleague, unhappy husband, and bitter ex-Army officer. And each and every one of them could be a pose.

He made the long walk to Van Zandt's house and strolled casually by on the other side of the street. The house on the corner was quiet and placid in the hot afternoon sun, apparently nothing or nobody moving behind the chintz-curtained windows. Susan's two boys were playing stick ball in the middle of the street but they were far too busy to notice him.

For the first hour nobody went into the house and nobody came out. Then a delivery boy drove up in a pickup truck and wrestled a huge box of groceries around to the back. He was gone for a few minutes and then came back whistling and counting some bills he had in his hands. Tanner watched him drive away. He'd be making other deliveries in the neighborhood and chances were the next one wouldn't be far away.

It wasn't. It was right in the next block.

The kid was perhaps seventeen, with a sallow face and hunched shoulders and wearing a dirty white apron with a green smear of celery leaf still clinging to it. When he talked, the gold braces on his teeth bobbed up and down and glinted in the sun.

"Yeah, they're regular customers. I deliver maybe once, twice a week. What's it to you?"

"What do you know about them?"

The boy climbed into the truck. "What the hell you trying to pull?"

Tanner took out his wallet and flashed his Naval Intelligence card. The boy shrugged. "All right, what d'ya want to know? But I'm warning you, I don't know a helluva lot."

"How long have you been delivering to them?"

"About a month. I got the job a little before school was out."

"Do they seem different at all from when you first started?"

The boy unwrapped a stick of chewing gum and folded it into his mouth. "I don't know. The old lady has always been pretty decent to me. Gives me coffee and tips me every now and then—she's getting pretty regular about that lately. I guess the old man is a holy terror. He used to be in the Army or something and he runs the house like he was running a division. They really snap to when he hollers. All he ever says to me is 'Put it here' or 'Put it there.'"

"Did you know John Olson when he lived with them?"

The boy's eyes opened wide for a moment. "I heard about him, I read about it in the paper. I never met him at all."

"Did the Professor and his wife ever mention him?"

"Yeah, the old lady once complained that he was nuts about strawberry jam and she was having to shell out too much for it. Outside of that, I don't remember either one of them ever saying anything about him."

"And they haven't changed a bit since Olson was killed?"

The boy shook his head. "I wouldn't say so. The house looks a lot different, though."

"How do you mean?"

"You know—new refrigerator and they got new linoleum on the floor and a freezer on the back porch. If you were me, you'd notice those things a lot. They'll be taking more frozen stuff now and less canned goods. Easier stuff for the store to pack."

Tanner started to walk away. "Thanks for your trouble." Olson had died and now the Van Zandts were living it up. . . .

The man in the local meat market was less cooperative. He was a big, hefty German, balding and with arms that Tanner couldn't have spanned with both hands.

"Yeah, she buys her meat in here all the time. Good customer, they got a family."

"She been buying more than usual lately?"

The butcher looked at him as if he were a pork chop in the display case. "You the police? If not, go peddle your papers some other place or I'll call the cops."

Tanner shrugged and walked out. He got more for his money at the beauty shop two blocks away.

The owner was a thin, hawk-nosed woman with graying hair neatly coiffed in bangs and a print dress that looked loose and comfortable.

"Susan Van Zandt? Oh my yes, she's one of my very steadiest customers. A really wonderful woman—you know she's married to a professor at the university. Why do you ask?"

Tanner lowered his voice to a confidential tone. "I'd like some information."

"Well, really, we're not in the habit of giving out information. . . . Is something wrong?" The birdlike eyes were glittering with curiosity.

"Should there be?"

A flutter of her hands and a quick glance at the curtained booths behind her where the dryers were. "Well, I really don't know. Just what was it you wanted to talk about?"

"I wondered if there has been any change in Mrs. Van Zandt. How she dresses, how she acts, that sort of thing."

A pursing of the mouth. "She's a really stunning dresser." Pause. "She didn't *use* to be, you know. She has a difficult figure to dress exactly right. Sort of an in-between—not slim and not exactly a stylish stout. You can get fitted, of course, but it costs a little more—special tailoring—and I imagine the Van Zandts didn't have the money." Another pause. "Apparently *that's* changed now."

"How do you mean?"

"My dear, you don't have to look at the labels to know where a woman is buying her clothes! I don't know how she does it but she's spending at least twice as much for her outfits as she used to. And when she comes in here! It used to be just a wave and a set and now it's everything!"

Tanner nodded agreeably and made little notes on a sheet of scratch paper. "You're being very helpful. How would you say she's changed personally?"

A slight frown. "Well, you know, I think there was a time when she and the Professor didn't get along very well. Sometimes she used to come in here and actually be *mean* to the girls. She's much different now. So self-assured, so confident, so . . . well, *content.*"

The same shiver went through Tanner that went through him when he scratched his fingernails across a blackboard. He folded the scrap of paper and put it away.

"You've been very helpful, Miss. Thanks a lot."

She looked disappointed.

"Aren't you going to tell me something? I mean, this wouldn't be perhaps a . . . divorce matter?"

"No," he said quietly. "It's much more serious than that. You might say it involves life and death."

"Well, *really!*"

And the funny thing, he thought outside, was that the old girl had the idea he was kidding.

He spent the rest of the afternoon interviewing other people in the neighborhood without too much success. The Van Zandts had kept pretty much to themselves. The shopkeepers were aware that they were spending a lot more money lately but most of them weren't too talkative about it.

By nightfall he was back in the Loop. He had the evening to kill until Nordlund showed up and then they had to map out a campaign against Van Zandt. He had a hunch that with Van they were on the wrong trail, but there had to be some reason for Van's sudden wealth. Would Adam Hart make such a suspicious move? Probably not, but then . . .

He ate in a little shoo-in restaurant on Washington and took in a movie. By the time he got out it was after ten and the streets were filled with the Thursday-night shift of joy seekers.

He walked down Randolph past the public library and ducked into the IC station to buy a paper. He'd scan it and see what the news was and if there was anything on Karl and then it would be time to meet Nordlund.

The story about Grossman was buried on the inside, an inch and a half of type on page nine. It didn't mention him by name; the body hadn't been identified. A fat man, about forty, found dead in an alleyway just off Rush Street. He had been wearing an unpressed brown suit, black shoes, white shirt and regimental-striped tie. Cause of death was unknown but the police had found no marks of violence.

It didn't *have* to be Grossman, Tanner thought, then realized he was kidding himself. A fat man who had wandered into an alley and died there. Like Olson had sat down in his room and died.

No marks of violence.

Of course not.

There would be nobody to mourn him. Nobody to claim the body. Nobody who would miss him. Karl's own family didn't even remember him.

He walked slowly out the entrance and recognized Nordlund standing in front of one of the library pillars. He handed him the paper. "Grossman's dead."

Nordlund read the squib in silence. For a moment Tanner was nettled, then knew there was really nothing that could be said. He dug his pipe out of his pocket and lit up, standing back in the shadows of the pillar and watching the people hurry by on the sidewalk a few feet away.

"I've checked up on Van Zandt. He's spending too much money lately."

"Where'd he get it?"

"I wish I knew."

"It doesn't sound like . . . Hart."

"No, it doesn't. But then it'd be a little difficult for us to second-guess Hart, wouldn't it?" He paused. "What about DeFalco?"

Nordlund frowned. "I don't know. His neighbors haven't

seen him around for the last week. I don't know what the score is but he seems to have done a fairly complete fade-out."

DeFalco. Hart. A fade-out didn't make sense. It was suspicious and Adam wasn't the type who would do anything obviously suspicious.

"If we last long enough," Nordlund said, "I think we might be safe."

"How do you figure that?"

"Somebody's bound to start investigating."

That was true, Tanner thought, but how soon? One member of the committee had been murdered—that was a local matter. One had been run over by a truck. Several had disappeared, if you counted Karl's death as a disappearance in the eyes of the local police. The local police would be in an uproar. But the national government? No reports were being filed to Washington, but it was summer and the committee was comatose then anyway. Some department head might put two and two together in a few days and get worried. But not right now. Not today.

"You're probably right, Commander. Somebody will probably start investigating. I figure in about a week. And we don't have that long."

"So what do we do? Just stand here?"

"We'll go after Van Zandt tomorrow. There's nothing more we can do tonight anyway."

"Professor?"

"What?"

Nordlund sounded a little reluctant. "Do you think it's such a wise idea to separate for the night again? If we had stayed together before, maybe Grossman would still be alive."

"That's right," Tanner said dryly. "He might. And on the other hand, all three of us might be dead."

Hesitantly: "I suppose that makes sense. Do we meet here again tomorrow?"

"Ten o'clock, same as today."

Tanner watched Nordlund walk down the steps and disappear into the entranceway of the station. He couldn't blame

Nordlund for being scared, for wanting to stick together for the night. Everybody hates to die, he thought. But most of all they hate to die without friends and relatives around.

Everybody hates to die alone.

17

TANNER walked down the library steps and lost himself in the crowd on the sidewalk. He hadn't been quite truthful in saying there was nothing that could be done that night. But then, it wouldn't have been very smart to reveal *all* his plans. What Nordlund didn't know, Nordlund would never be able to tell . . . someone else.

It was risky, he thought. It was dangerous and foolhardy, but maybe tonight was the perfect time to pay the Van Zandts a visit.

He stole a car that was parked along a side street and drove out towards the Van Zandts, parking a good four blocks from their home. He checked his pistol, then left the car and cut through a back yard into an alley. He made a slow, cautious approach to the Van Zandt home, not wanting to stumble over tin cans or bottles or anything else that would make noise. When he was opposite the Van Zandt back yard, he moved quietly into the shadows of the garage and watched.

There was a light on in the kitchen, somebody was home. Midnight and perhaps the Van Zandts were taking a coffee break from their TV set. He glanced at the street. There were no cars parked in the driveway, the Van Zandts weren't entertaining any company.

He silently lifted the latch on the fence gate and padded quietly up the walk. For a minute he was worried that the porch steps would creak or that the screen door would be locked. The door opened easily and he stepped quietly into the shadows of the porch. The noise he did make wasn't very loud; he brushed against a skate and it rolled a little across the floor. There were footsteps inside and Susan Van Zandt opened the kitchen door wide, the yellow light flooding past her.

"I thought sure . . ."

He stepped out of the darkness and into the kitchen. Susan's hand flew to her mouth and he could hear the scream gathering in her lungs.

He shoved the Beretta against her bathrobe—a new robe this time, black and shocking pink—and said, "Please be quiet, Susan. No screaming, no hysterics. Now call your husband. In your normal voice."

She stood there a moment longer, her chest heaving as she muffled the screams that wanted to bubble out, then turned on her heel and walked back into the kitchen. New pink-silk mules, too, Tanner thought.

He had been in the kitchen once before. He didn't recognize it now. The delivery boy had understated it. There was a new freezer and a new refrigerator. There were also new cabinets and a new range that had as many dials as the instrument panel of a jet plane. He could see part way into the hall. The worn carpeting had been replaced by a deep, carved-pile rug that stretched from wall to wall.

Susan didn't have time to call her husband. Van Zandt came

walking into the kitchen carrying the evening paper and holding a glass of milk. He was wearing a new wine-red smoking
jacket that Tanner knew he couldn't have touched for anything
less than a few hundred dollars and probably more.

He didn't see Tanner at first. "I thought I heard somebody
out here, Sue. I . . ."

The glass slipped from his hand and shattered on the floor
and warm milk ran all over the new linoleum.

Tanner motioned with his pistol. "Over there, Van. Sit at
the table and put your hands on top."

"I . . . don't carry firearms."

"Just do what I say, Van. You, too, Sue. Over there."

"You're making a mistake, Bill." Her voice was low and
throaty; she had recovered from the first shock of seeing him on
the porch.

"I don't think so."

She sat down, her eyes watching him warily, and he knew
she was the more dangerous of the two.

"All I want you to do, Van, is to answer some questions.
For example: how did John Olson die?"

Van Zandt cleared his throat. "You ought to know. The police say you killed him."

"You know better than that. I think you were there when it
happened, maybe you even saw him the very moment life flickered out. Maybe that's what did it, maybe you were scared. I'd
rather think that than anything else."

They didn't say anything but just stared at him.

He waved the gun at them. "Oh, come on now. Don't clam
up—let's hear the details. Or maybe I should tell them to you?
I won't fill you in on the background. You know all about Adam
Hart, the gypsy boy from Brockton. Maybe you know too much
about him. If I were you, I'd worry about that. You know how
he kills and you know that he held John Olson in the palm of
his hand and then just squeezed the life out of him. You had a
head start on the rest of us, Van. Olson lived with you. You
knew he was running downhill and you must have been curious
as to why. You started your investigation early, long before that

Saturday morning." He paused. "You saw Olson die. You saw him sweat and squirm and you saw him clutch at his chest when his breathing stopped and you saw his life slip away when his heart beat ceased."

Susan flinched and Tanner leaned towards her. "What's the matter, am I getting too graphic? Offending your finer sensibilities? Come off it, Susan. You care a lot about your own family but you don't give a damn for anybody else. When I talked to you about John ten days ago you showed as much emotion about his death as you would about a blade of grass that had been stepped on."

Van Zandt had gained back some of his courage. "You're rambling," he said sarcastically.

Tanner turned the pistol slightly. "I don't want any crap, Van. I mean it. What I'm driving at is that John Olson didn't just curl up and die, like everybody thinks he did. Like you told the police he did—though that doesn't matter now. But John Olson had been used by Adam Hart a hundred times before, and there's nothing like fighting the devil you know. It wasn't easy for Hart to control him this last time. Olson didn't win his fight but I think he managed to get out one scream, didn't he? Maybe two. Enough to waken you and Susan and maybe enough to bother the neighbors. But when they came over you told them it was nothing and a few days later they had forgotten all about it. Naturally. Isn't that just about the size of it?"

Van Zandt's voice was thick. "You're guessing. It's all guesses."

Tanner nodded. "That's right. It's all guesses. And I make some bum ones. I even thought for a while that *you* might be Adam Hart. Silly, wasn't it? Adam Hart is a monster but you two are something worse." He ran his hand across his forehead; it was wet and it wasn't all from heat and exhaustion. His breathing was ragged and he knew he was running a fever. "You saw Olson die, and you guessed how. It shouldn't have been hard for you, Van. He lived here with you, you had already started investigating, and you were studying him at the meeting like he was a bug under glass. After the demonstration you put two and two together and you must have been a lot sharper at it than I was. Maybe you even helped Scott with his dossiers. You guessed who Adam Hart was and then you did something that turns my stomach."

Susan wasn't looking at him but was staring down at the table. Oddly enough, Van seemed more relaxed, not at all worried; the slight shadow of a smile was flickering over his face.

"You sold out," Tanner said thinly. "For money. For the filthy green. And Adam Hart accepted because he realized that even he could use allies, that you might be valuable. He could have controlled you directly but that would have taken time and effort and unwilling servants are never as useful as those who are enthusiastic about their position. Maybe you fingered Professor Scott, maybe it was you who told Hart that Grossman's weakest spot was his family. Maybe you even sicced him on to Marge, knowing what it would do to me. You'd be good at that, you're a psychologist. You'd complement Hart." He stopped, feeling lightheaded and exhausted. "You sold out everybody you knew, you sold out humanity. And for what?"

Van Zandt's smile was broader now. "You're a fool, Tanner. Always were and always will be. We didn't invent Adam Hart, we didn't make him like Frankenstein made his monster. But he's here and anybody who knows it and doesn't realize that the world will dance to his tune if he wants it to is stupid. You know it, I know it. That's one of the things they teach you when you're a military man. To know when your position is indefensible. And what's the old saying? 'When you can't lick 'em jine 'em.' I jumped on the bandwagon. Maybe I'm a little ahead of the rest of the crowd but that's my good fortune. Within a couple of months that bandwagon's going to be pretty crowded."

He shook his head and looked at Tanner sadly. "You value your fellowman too highly, William. They're intelligent cattle, that's all. I think that Adam wants to run the world and when he does, people will be a lot healthier, happier, and better cared for."

"When Adam's running the stockyard, the cattle will be watered and fed and sprayed every week to get rid of the bugs, that it, Van?"

Susan was still staring steadily at the table, a Mona Lisa expression on her face, and it bothered him. A table set for three. Some people set their table late at night so they wouldn't have to worry about it early in the morning.

Then it hit him.

A table for three.

Why wasn't it set for just the two of them, or if their children were going to be eating at the same time, four?

Three.

It had been set for that night, he thought suddenly. A table for three. For Susan and Harold and Adam. A snack before turning in, a little lighthearted conversation with a monster to prove to him over and over and over that they were really on his side. Maybe talk far into the night so they wouldn't have to spend so much time lying in bed, alone with their consciences.

A table for three and they had been waiting for the other party when he had walked in.

He abruptly backed into the hallway leading to the front part of the house.

"Where's he staying, Van?"

Van Zandt looked at him with grinning triumph playing peek-a-boo in his small, deep-set eyes. "Where's who, William?"

"Eddy DeFalco, Van. You know—Adam Hart."

18

"**I WOULDN'T** know," Van Zandt said quietly. "I wouldn't tell you if I did."

"I watched Scott get his and I read all about Karl dying in an alleyway. I don't have the qualms I used to, Van." Tanner's hand tensed. "You're a free agent. You don't have the compulsion not to talk. Where is he?"

Van Zandt's smile faded. His hands on the table top trembled slightly. Then there was something else in his eyes besides fear, the barest shadow of relief.

Tanner felt it at the same instant, like he had felt it once before in Petey's apartment building. The presence at the side gate lifting the latch, the presence walking up the sidewalk.

The third guest was arriving.

"You're lucky, Van," Tanner whispered. "At least for

a few minutes. I don't think Adam's going to be very happy with you."

He turned and ran through the house to the front door, then hesitated in the darkness and looked out the front window. There were no cars out front, nobody was waiting.

He eased the door open, held the lock so it wouldn't make a noise snapping shut, and closed it gently behind him. He ran two doors down, cutting through a back yard and standing in the shadows to watch. He could see through the yards to the Van Zandt corner lot and the street that ran along the side of their house. The front door banged open and he could see a figure standing on the steps. Adam Hart, seeing if he were still around. Then the figure went back in and the door slammed shut behind it.

Tanner glanced at the kitchen window. Only the little lamp on the kitchen table was lit now and it cast fantastic shadows on the windows. He could make out three distorted figures, one of which was gesticulating angrily. Then all motion stopped and the three shadows were carved in black and gray.

The light on the table suddenly went out and the scream, when it came, was more of a whimper than a scream. Tanner felt a slight tingling in the air, as if he had been touched very briefly by a bubble of something intangible that had pulsed outward from the house.

Hart must have been angry because the Van Zandts had failed to keep him there. And he must have realized that the Van Zandts were living not wisely, but too well—and too recently. If and when the government looked into the case, there would be questions. And Van Zandt could supply the answers.

So there had to be . . . *fury*.

There was a flickering, lurid light in the kitchen now. It caught a shadow that danced around the walls, plucking at the cabinets and tearing at the refrigerator and pulling things out, something that hammered at the range and smashed the wooden chairs. There was the faint, muffled sound of smashing china and all the while the light grew brighter and stronger.

Tanner watched, unable to turn away. Minutes passed and

now the flames were eating at the chintz curtains and there was the sound of popping windows. A moment later the screen door slammed and a figure in a trench coat and a slouch hat ran down the stairs and over to an automobile on the side street. It got in and the car roared away.

The neighbors would turn in an alarm, Tanner thought, but it would be too late. The house was frame and it burned far too fast . . . like a house had back in Brockton years before. Van Zandt's home would burn to the ground. For some reason the coroner would forget to make an investigation and there would be no mention of it in the papers. The wreckers would move in tomorrow and by the end of the week the lot would be leveled and rolled and planted in grass. The neighbors wouldn't be able to tell you who had lived there, the butcher would only look puzzled if you mentioned the name, the woman in the beauty parlor would say, "Well, really, I've never heard of them," and the delivery boy would give you a stony stare and tell you to go to hell.

Van Zandt and Susan and their two children. At best, they would cause a faint baffled frown if anybody who had known them ran across the name again.

Permanent erasure, not even a memory left.

He walked quickly through the alley, keeping to the shadows of the garages and the back fences.

There was a full moon and the stars were very bright in the sky.

He dodged from shadow to shadow and waited a moment before sprinting across the open streets to make sure that nobody was watching. The avenues were empty and silent—the whole city was indoors, listening to the radio or making themselves midnight snacks or tossing restlessly in hot, stuffy little bedrooms. He clung to the alleys and when he had to use the streets he tried to keep in the puddling shadows between the street lamps or run silently past the houses, ducking in the shadows of trees whenever a car passed.

Four blocks back to his car seemed like four miles.

He drove downtown and parked in the belt of slums that

girdled the Loop. It was risky to stay with the stolen car but he was too sick to leave it and spend another night running. It was two in the morning and he was shaking with exhaustion and burning up with fever. He crawled into the back seat and stared out at the lamplit darkness, cradling his Beretta in his lap and waiting. He couldn't keep his eyes from closing. He'd doze for a few minutes and each time wake up shaking with the chills.

Friday morning came very slowly.

He had breakfast in a cheap cafeteria, sitting in a corner so people wouldn't notice his whiskered face and his rumpled clothing. An hour to go before the library opened. Another hour or so before Nordlund was due.

And then what?

He dawdled over his coffee until after nine, paid his tab, and left. The reading room of the library was already comfortably crowded with students and bums who had come in for a little shut-eye, safe in the knowledge that the librarians were softer-hearted than cops and wouldn't throw them out. He spent an hour pretending that he was absorbed in a magazine, then went out to the lobby.

Nordlund was waiting for him, his eyes red-rimmed and his suit rumpled and worn. The Navy man hadn't done so well that night either, Tanner thought, and somehow he got a small twinge of perverse pleasure out of it.

"I see we were both lucky," Nordlund said.

"It could have been worse." The girl in the information booth was staring at them and Tanner started for the door. "Let's go over to the park and sit down."

They found a bench on the other side of the Boulevard and Nordlund collapsed into it, hooking his elbows over the back and letting his head sag back. His eyes closed. "What are we going to do about Van Zandt?"

"Nothing. He's dead."

Nordlund froze, his head still back and his eyes still closed. His lips formed the silent syllable, "How?"

"Last night. Hart got him. Like Olson. Like Grossman. Van Zandt and his whole family." He took a ragged breath. "Don't feel sorry for him. Van was working with him, working with him all the time."

People walking up the Boulevard stared at them and quickly looked away. A cop strolling by didn't even glance at them. Like the library, the park was in limits for bums.

Nordlund's voice was nervous. "That doesn't leave many, does it?"

"DeFalco's it."

Nordlund leaned forward and held his head with his hands. He looked like he was going to cry. "And now that we know it, what are we going to do about it? What are we going to do, Tanner? This guy is superman—what the hell are *we* doing chasing him?"

"Don't overestimate him. He makes mistakes, he gets panicky, too."

"He makes mistakes?" Nordlund asked bitterly. "Here you sit, dirty and sick, and there he goes, free as a bird. And you think he makes mistakes?"

"I'm still alive," Tanner said quietly.

Nordlund took a deep breath and let it out in a sob of resignation. His hands were shaking. "Okay, Professor, I'm still with you. But what do we do now?"

He had to consider it logically, Tanner thought, to ignore the fact that he was sick and burning with fever. He had solved a major problem: he knew who Hart was. But now that he knew, what was he going to do about it?

And then he thought he had part of the answer. Hart had planted evidence to hang John Olson's murder on him and he, Tanner, had obliged by running as soon as he had heard about it. But maybe that was a game that two could play at.

"Maybe we could frame Hart—for Olson's murder."

A tired laugh. "You're crazy, Professor. They want *you* for the killing."

"But *I* didn't kill Olson, DeFalco did—Hart did."

"The police won't believe it—all the evidence is against you."

"Nobody's admitted the crime, Commander. The murderer

wasn't caught red-handed, nobody saw him do it. Without an admission of guilt, and with the supposed murderer a formerly respected member of the community, all the evidence in the world would still leave a lingering doubt."

Nordlund shook his head. "It'd be your word against his. You haven't got the time to manufacture any evidence against DeFalco, and if you turned yourself in and insisted you were innocent you know damn' well what would happen. You need an assist."

Eddy DeFalco, Tanner thought. Clean-cut, young, personable. And he should be for he was actually Adam Hart—and nobody could help but love Adam. But now maybe Hart had made a mistake. Hart was probably spending just as much time and effort in looking for him as he was in trying to avoid being found. Maybe Hart was superman but he couldn't be in two places at once. While Hart was out looking, DeFalco couldn't possibly be home.

He had been on the run for the last two weeks, Tanner thought, which also meant that Hart had been on the run—and DeFalco must have had to disappear for long lengths of time.

"I think I might have my assist, Commander. When the police finally agreed that it was murder, didn't Lieutenant Crawford ask that none of you leave town? Since you all knew me, you were all valuable witnesses."

"One of his men dropped around every night to bring me up to date, too, but so what?"

"He came around to see that you were still on the string, Commander. Now do you see it? DeFalco's disappeared—Crawford will at least be suspicious. And maybe that gives us an in." He stood up and started walking west, across the Boulevard.

Nordlund caught up with him and grabbed his arm. "How does that tie up? Where are you going now?"

Tanner felt lightheaded and weak and a little tired of explanations. He couldn't understand why Nordlund couldn't see what was perfectly obvious to him. "If Crawford is suspicious of DeFalco now, it will take only a thread to tie him up to Olson, only a suggestion to make Crawford want to pick DeFalco up for questioning."

"And what if he does?" Nordlund said stiffly. "Everybody loves Adam, everybody will believe whatever he has to say."

Tanner didn't want to argue, he was getting to believe something now and he didn't want it spoiled, he didn't want it knocked down. "Hart won't run the risk of having three or four people question him at once, he won't run the risk of being questioned with a lie detector. A machine isn't flesh and blood, Commander—a machine won't love him!"

"So what are you going to do about it?"

Tanner started to laugh, then choked and spit phlegm into the gutter. "Adam Hart's off balance, Commander—and I'm going to push a little."

And then he added to himself: *if Adam doesn't catch me first.*

They turned west on Madison Street. Across the river, Madison, the business street, turned into West Madison, the street of forgotten dreams for the drunks and the bums. He picked a hole-in-the-wall tavern that was open and walked in past a balding man who was sweeping down.

What he wanted was slumped at a table in the back of the room, for the moment the only customer in the house, her head on her arms and her brick-red hair streaming over the sticky wooden table top.

"You got some money, Commander?"

Nordlund gave him some and Tanner threw the bills on the table and shook the woman roughly.

"Huh? Wassamatter?"

"You want to make a few bucks?"

Her eyes swam slowly to a focus and she tried to arch her back so her flabby breasts jutted out, then gave it up as a bad job. She put her head back on her arms. "Go 'way—it's too damned early in the morning. . . ."

Tanner added another bill.

"All you have to do is make a phone call."

She sat up and stared at the money. Tanner motioned to the bartender, who brought over a bottle of cheap wine. He set it on the table, just out of her reach.

She stood up, hanging tightly to the table for support, and squinted up at him. "Whaddya wan' me to do?"

He took her over to the pay phone and slapped her once, hard. Her head rocked back and the bleary look faded. *"Get your filthy hands offa me!"*

"Look, you don't sober up for five seconds it's no money and no wine, you get me?" He dropped a coin in the box and dialed a number. "All you have to do is say what I tell you to say and you'll get enough liquor to last you for a week."

She shrugged. Tanner listened intently to the phone, then nodded and whispered in her ear.

"I wanna speak to Lootenant Crawford," she said. Tanner put his hand over the mouthpiece as soon as she got done and waited for the reply. When he heard it, he whispered again.

"Never min' who it is, just gimme the Lootenant."

Pause.

"I got somethin' to tell you, Lootenant. Professor Tanner didn't—didn't kill Johnny Olson. DeFalco did."

Pause. She blinked her eyes and frowned, as if she were just starting to realize what she was doing. Tanner whispered urgently to her again.

"Never min'. Just say it was over . . . over me."

He hung up and helped her past the table where he scooped up the money and the bottle and gave it to her. She wanted to sit down. His fingers tightened on her fleshy arm and he pushed her to the door. "Not here," he said harshly. "Down the street. The cops'll be here in a minute—you wouldn't want them to catch you, would you?"

She shook free, blazing mad. "Gitcha goddamned paws offa me! And they don't have to look me up, I'm gonna tell 'em! You oughtta learn how to treat a lady like a . . . lady!" She started down the street, then suddenly turned and made a face at him, daring him to do anything about it.

Tanner shrugged and went back in to the bartender. He

took a bill out of his pocket. "You don't have to remember much, do you?"

The man took the money and folded it into a small, flat wad and slipped it into his watch pocket.

"I never seen you come in—I never seen you leave."

Outside, Nordlund said, "What if she goes to the police?"

"She won't go near one. And even if they pick her up an hour from now, it will be too late. She'll be too drunk to remember anything."

"The call she made—it was pretty crude."

Tanner's head felt warm and his stomach a little queasy. Nervous exhaustion had finally caught up with him; he wouldn't last another day.

"Maybe they'll believe it, maybe they won't Commander. It's only supposed to be a thread between DeFalco and Olson's murder—just enough to get the police a little interested."

Nordlund leaned against a lamppost and jammed his hands in his pockets. His face was expressionless. "And then what?"

"If you've got money enough, I think I'll get a shave," Tanner said slowly. "Maybe you ought to, too. And then we're going to deliver the body. We're going to call the police and tell them where they can find DeFalco."

"You know, I suppose."

Tanner shook his head. "No, I don't. But I know somebody who does. Hart's a logical man. He knows that DeFalco's absences will be suspicious. But the days don't have to be explained, and for the evenings he'll have an alibi. He spent the night with a girl friend. And five will get you ten that the girl friend is Rosemary O'Connor."

She had been a clerk in a woman's clothing store not far from the campus, or so the rumor went. Which meant she had left a trail and wouldn't be hard to find.

After he and Nordlund cleaned up, they started covering the shops in the campus area. By late afternoon they found the manager of the shop where Rosemary O'Connor had worked two years before. The manager was a prim, prissy little man who looked as delicate as the bow tie he wore.

"Oh yes, Miss O'Connor. I remember her quite well. She was in something of a scandal as I recall. Naturally we discharged her immediately." He eyed the two Naval Intelligence men speculatively.

"Do you know where she lived? Any files kept on her?"

"Yes, sir, I'm quite sure we still have them." He waved a wrist at a saleslady behind a nearby counter. "Miss Sherwood, the personnel record on Rosemary O'Connor, if you please." While they were waiting, he asked, "I know it's none of my business but is she wanted for something? I wouldn't doubt it if she was, of course."

Tanner didn't bother answering.

"Oh. I didn't mean to pry, you understand. Just curiosity."

"Of course."

The manager looked unhappy and then the salesgirl came up with the file folder marked *Rosemary O'Connor.* Tanner leafed through the contents. Home address and phone, which probably had been changed by now. The address was listed under her own name; she hadn't been living with her parents.

What interested him most was a letter from an insurance company, asking for a recommendation. It had been a stupid thing to do, he thought. She hadn't been likely to get a good recommendation from the shop. The carbon of their letter was attached and while it never said so in so many words, it left no doubt as to the kind of girl Rosemary was supposed to be.

He debated for a moment, and then dialed the phone number that was on the letterhead of the insurance company. They hadn't hired the girl, but they had kept her application on file. The address was a new one on the west side of the city.

If they hurried, Tanner thought, they could be waiting for her when she came home from work.

Her apartment was in a run-down section of town where the fire escapes made a rusty tracery against the deep blue sky. They waited in the tiny entranceway of the building, a cracked-tile cubbyhole where all the names over the mailboxes were scribbled in pencil.

When she walked in, Tanner didn't have to be introduced. She stopped and stared at them and he knew it was her. She wasn't an exceptionally pretty girl, which surprised him. Average height and maybe just a little too plump. Good skin and features, dark complexion, and black hair that was thick and a little too oily. The Irish in the family was all on her father's side, he thought. He could imagine her a few years in the future, cooking spaghetti and taking care of three or four kids.

A strictly average girl, passably pretty and attractive, fairly intelligent, who had once made a mistake she couldn't possibly have avoided. A patsy for Adam Hart.

He showed his card and jerked a thumb at Nordlund standing behind him. "We'd like to talk to you."

Her voice was cold. "Come on up." She led the way up the stairs to a dingy apartment with a colorless rug and a sofa where you could see the springs just under the worn upholstery. She took off her hat and turned to face them. "Well?"

"Do you know Eddy DeFalco?"

"You wouldn't be asking me if you didn't think so."

"Do you know where he's staying?"

"No."

"I think you're lying."

"That's your privilege."

He pointed to Nordlund. "We're with the government, Rose. We have to know."

"I don't have to tell you."

"You been going with Eddy very long, Rose?"

"Long enough."

"It's been a couple of years now, hasn't it?"

"If you knew the figures, why ask me?"

"You knew he was running around with other women, didn't you?"

"Yes, I knew it."

"And you still stuck with him?"

"Yes."

"Why?"

"That's a silly question, isn't it?"

"He got you into trouble, Rose. You lost your job over it."

"It was no great loss—it wasn't worth keeping."

"Where's he staying, Rose?"

"I told you I didn't know!"

"What would you do if I told you Eddy was a murderer?"

She stared at him. "I wouldn't believe it," she whispered.

"I'm sorry, Rose, but he is. The other night he killed an entire family."

She shook her head wildly, her eyes closed as if in pain. "No, no, no. You've got it all wrong! He's afraid of something, he's been running from somebody! He didn't kill anybody—he's been worried about somebody killing him!"

"It's been a front," Tanner said gently. "And you've been part of it."

"*I don't believe it!*"

"Where does he spend the nights, Rose?"

"Right here, with me, where'd you think?"

"Got any idea where he is right now?"

"Look, I'm not going to tell you anything. . . ."

He snapped and was suddenly towering over her. "I'm not looking for him just because he's your boy friend and I don't give a damn how many times you went to bed with him! Maybe you'd like to know that Eddy DeFalco isn't Eddy DeFalco at all, maybe you'd like to know he isn't even human! Maybe you'd like to know that for the last two years he's been masquerading and you've been nothing but part of his costume!"

She started to cry, tight little tears that trickled reluctantly out of the corners of her eyes. "*I won't tell you a thing, not a goddamned thing! Go ahead and do anything you want to!*"

"Nordlund, get her purse."

Nordlund disappeared and came back a moment later. Rosemary suddenly stopped crying, her eyes wary. "What do you want with my purse?"

Tanner opened it up without answering and dumped the

contents on the sofa. Rosemary made a lunge for it but Nordlund held her back.

Rouge and lipstick and a cheap little compact. A carefully
folded handkerchief and a little perfumed sachet of rose leaves.
Keys and a small tin of aspirin and a broken pencil. An address
book. And tickets. Tickets in four different colors to the city's
amusement park.

Chicago's fun park, the largest in the world, over seventy
acres of roller coasters and ferris wheels and lemonade stands.
A different colored ticket for every day. Tickets that had been
bought for different rides and then not used and stuffed away in
her purse. Tickets that still had a crisp, new feel so they must
have been purchased fairly recently.

"How often do you meet him there, Rose? Every night?
And you don't actually come back here at all, do you? He sees
you for an hour or so and then he disappears, doesn't he?"

She crumpled then. She sagged into the chair next to the
couch, her eyes closed and the sobs shaking her apart. *"We do!
Honest to God, we come back here . . . every . . . night!"*

He had him, Tanner thought. One more faked call to Crawford and the police would be in the amusement park looking for
DeFalco/Hart—who would have no idea that the police were
after him.

"Don't try to leave, Rose. There's a policeman at the front
and one stationed in the alley. You can't help Eddy now anyway." It was a lie but it would be enough to keep her from trying to warn DeFalco.

Even after he had closed the door, he could still hear her
sobbing. She loved DeFalco, he thought, and wondered if Hart
had forced her to. Probably not—it wouldn't have made a bit
of difference to her how much of a monster he was.

19

IT was the smells that hit him first. The sickly sweet smell of cotton candy and caramel corn and sugar waffles, mixed with the faint exhaust odors from the diesel engines that drove the rides. The locker-room odor of thousands of people eating and milling about in the open and the sticky smell of Coke and root beer and orange pop. The stink of hot dogs and raw onions and the sharp, rancid odor of buttered popcorn.

And the noises. The cries of the barkers and the drifting shreds of conversation from the crowds.

"... *your luck folks, hit the milk bottles* ..."

"... *show the little girl how strong you are* ..."

"... *wanna go on the rolly coaster* ..."

"... *three for a quarter, try your luck* ..."

"... *two tickets for the Tunnel of Love* ..."

"*. . . got sick all over me,* your *son . . .*"

Nordlund had bought himself a hamburger and was eating it, leaning over slightly so the drippings wouldn't hit his shirt.

"Got any idea how they're going to work it, Professor?"

Tanner shrugged. "I suspect Crawford will leave only one exit open and the police will watch as the people leave."

"They'll have a tough time with this crowd."

"Maybe."

Nordlund took a sip from his bottle of pop. "What's to keep the police from running you in?"

"In the first place I'm not going to walk up and introduce myself, and in the second they're not looking for me right now."

"Professor . . ." Nordlund paused. "Why couldn't Hart go right over the fence, if he wanted?"

"Why should he? He doesn't even know the police are looking for him yet. He's still carrying on the masquerade, he's still Edward DeFalco, waiting for Rosemary O'Connor to show up. And if worse came to worse, the park isn't so big it couldn't be surrounded."

"Any reason why he can't walk right out? Different people see Hart in different ways, who would recognize him?"

"That gets the same answer as the other. He doesn't know anybody is looking for him, he's still Eddy DeFalco."

Nordlund finished off the hamburger and wiped his thin fingers on a greasy paper napkin. "How does it feel to be winning for a change?"

"It isn't over yet, Commander."

He walked slowly down the midway, listening to the crowds and catching the expectant hush as the roller coasters crept to the top of their hills, the ratchets clicking sharply beneath the cars, and then the thundering roar as the cars caromed down the incline with the shrieks of their riders cutting through the night.

Something wet splashed on his face and he glanced up. Dark clouds had rolled in over the moon and a sharp wind was rattling through the leaves of the trees. It looked like the weather was going to break and there was going to be a heavy summer thunder-shower, one where it would rain torrents and the sheet lightning would look like fireworks.

Some of the people on the midway felt the raindrops and started to drift toward the exits. Tanner glanced at his watch—the men at the gate would be checking now. And it was just about time that DeFalco/Hart was leaving. He would have gotten tired of waiting for Rosemary to show up. She wouldn't have been meeting him much before eight—she got out of work at five-thirty, give her time to eat and dress—and he wouldn't have waited for her much beyond eight-thirty or nine. About an hour together, usually, and then they would have split up.

DeFalco would have had more serious duties for the rest of the evening. An hour to keep up the pretenses with Rosemary and then back to stalking the streets of the city as Adam Hart.

He stopped at a shooting gallery and bought a quarter's worth of ammunition from the woman who ran it. She absently handed him the gun, frowning at the people hurrying past the booth towards the exit.

"Looks like we'll close early tonight."

Tanner aimed the gun, spattered the targets at the back, and handed it back to her. "Bad night, huh?"

She leaned over the counter and lowered her voice confidentially. "Y'know, there's a rumor going around that they got a murderer trapped in here."

Tanner felt cold. However it had started, it might tip off Hart that something was up.

"You believe it?"

She racked the rifle and laughed. "Why not? Gives a body a little excitement to look forward to."

Tanner laughed and walked away.

He hadn't taken more than half a dozen steps when he heard it. It was dim and faint and sounded like nothing more than a car backfiring or somebody at another shooting gallery a few hundred feet away. He turned to Nordlund. "You hear that?"

Nordlund nodded. "It sounded like a shot."

Tanner glanced around. The midway was almost deserted and the lights had started to go out in the different booths. The rain was spattering down now, hitting the crumpled candy wrappers and the remains of ice-cream cones and the little bits of bun that littered the ground. A few concessionnaires in raincoats were rolling down the canvas in front of their booths.

And then people started to come back up the midway, coming back from the exit like water backing up in a drain. A few were running and looking over their shoulders, others were scrambling off the midway itself into the shadows of the booths and the different rides.

Another shot from the direction of the exit.

Tanner smiled crookedly. What was it that Karl had once said? They were like dogs trying to catch the dog catcher? But it had worked. Hart had panicked and had used a pistol. The police wouldn't have shot him, they wanted him merely for questioning. So it must have been the other way around. A brief moment of panic and Hart had lost.

A policeman was running down the midway. *"Get off the midway, everybody off the midway!"*

Tanner and Nordlund moved back into the shadows of a concession booth and sat on a bench. Nordlund turned up his collar and pulled down his hat to keep off the blowing rain. His eyes closed and his chest started to move with an easy, deep rhythm.

"Don't you want to watch, Commander?"

Nordlund reluctantly opened one eye. "There's nothing we can do one way or the other. And I'm so beat I can't stand up."

A mile away, Tanner could hear the first, faint cries of the sirens. The reinforcements were coming up and the man hunt was about to begin.

The man stepped out of the shadows two hundred feet away and started sprinting down the midway. There was a shot and the man staggered and for a fraction of a second Tanner was looking at the wild, tortured face of Edward DeFalco. Then DeFalco was past him, twisting and dodging and running faster than Tanner had ever seen a man run before.

Then there were other men on the midway, running and ducking into the shadows and firing after the fleeing figure. DeFalco turned in mid-stride and flame spurted from a pistol he held. A policeman far down the midway screamed and dropped to the ground. There was a fusillade of shots and De-Falco stumbled again, then was up and running. He wasn't going to die easy, Tanner thought.

DeFalco suddenly ducked between two concession stands and was lost to sight. Tanner could see the spot where he had disappeared; the space between the stands was nothing but shadows and darkness.

Other people were filling the midway now. The police, lugging rifles and riot guns, and the surging, curious crowd. Then other policemen were blocking off the area and holding the crowds back.

Tanner felt cold and wet. He sneezed and tried to wrap his collar tighter around his throat. Nordlund was at his side, offering him a cigarette. "This has turned into a pretty big man hunt, hasn't it, Professor?"

"They're hunting a pretty big man." He didn't feel a great deal like talking. The tension had built up within him and it was fighting with the fatigue that was making him sick. He knew when it was all over that he would lie down and collapse some place for forty-eight hours.

A whisper started to float through the crowd. *"The fun house—they've trapped him in the fun house!"*

The crowd surged down a street just off the midway and Tanner followed it. The crowd packed itself around the fun house in a huge arc. It was a real professional setup, Tanner thought. The fun house was surrounded on all sides, there were spotlights on the entrances, and Crawford was talking over a small, portable loudspeaker. His words sounded high and querulous in the mounting wind.

And then silence. The sound of the rain pelting down and the breathing of the crowd and little snatches of mumbled conversation. The lights and the trees and the big wire trash baskets etched sharply against the night. The gaudy front of the fun house, the face of a gigantic clown with a bulbous nose and a grinning mouth for an entranceway, the red paint and the gilt gleaming wetly in the lights.

The police threw in tear gas and half a dozen men with masks disappeared into the grinning mouth.

They almost missed DeFalco when he made a break for it. Even with the lights, a little window in a corner, about six feet above the ground, was in the shadow. It opened noiselessly and a man wriggled silently out.

"There he goes!"

DeFalco ran straight down the midway, running the gamut of the guns and the lights. The guns chattered and he stumbled, then somehow made it to his feet and was running like the wind. A hundred yards, two hundred yards, and he was running through the thin stretch of grass that separated him from the wooden framework of one of the roller coasters.

The lights and the cars and the hunters moved after him, flowing down the street like a gigantic amoeba. In the shadows of the wooden framework, a figure worked its way rapidly towards the top, leaping from beam to beam with an agility that far surpassed that of any human being.

". . . lights, get the lights . . ."

". . . there, at the top . . ."

". . . can't miss, all over . . ."

". . . all over!"

A scattering of shots from the figure high in the framework. Then the lights were on him, first one picking him out and clinging tenaciously and then the others until the whole roller-coaster framework was bathed in light. DeFalco was caught in the center, like a fly in a web. Somehow Tanner thought he heard the man scream, *"Oh my God!"*

Then the riot guns caught him and he fell and the guns still clung, their invisible fingers plucking at him while he was still in the air. He hit the ground and bounced and it was all over.

All over.

The crowd surged forward. Tanner got near enough to catch a glimpse of the thing on the grass and felt sick. An ambulance drove up and two men with a blanket and a stretcher took away what was left of Edward DeFalco. The telltale stains lingered for a while in the rain and then were diluted and dissolved and washed away and the green of the grass showed through, the mud at its roots looking a little richer.

Tanner stood in the rain and stared for long minutes, then turned and walked slowly back to the overhang of a concession booth. The spotlights were winking out one by one and the brilliant white of the roller-coaster framework faded to oyster gray and then a dirty gray and then almost disappeared entirely against the black sky, just a shadow in the darkness.

Men stripped apart the riot guns, put them back into cases, and slung them into waiting automobiles. There was the gentle purr of motors and one after another the cars drove to the entrance. The crowd was breaking into little groups and heading for the exit. The amoeba was flowing away from the park now, out into the city, to split up and go back to its various homes and stations and garages.

She had loved him, Tanner thought. *She didn't care what kind of a monster he was. And she had cried and said he couldn't have done it.*

Somebody said something to him and he turned blindly around. It was Crawford. "Commander Nordlund said you were over here, Professor. We'll need a statement from you in the morning, of course."

"Certainly." Tanner started walking through the beating rain towards the exit.

He didn't see the girl at first, didn't even know she was there until she had thrown herself on him and was sobbing in his ear. "Bill, Bill, I'm so glad you're safe!"

Marge. The police must have asked her down to help identify DeFalco.

"Bill, it's been a nightmare!" She stood there in the rain, expectantly, waiting for him to take her into his arms or kiss her or walk arm in arm into the sunset. Sunshine and health and the faint odor of "Tweed" perfume.

A new Chevvy pulled up and Commander Nordlund stuck his head out the window. "Hey, kids, Crawford lent me a car—can I give you a lift?"

Tanner walked over like he was in a dream.

"It's all over, isn't it?" he said stupidly.

Nordlund looked at him sharply. "You feel all right?"

"Yes, I feel all right." Tanner shivered. "It's all over, isn't it? No more running, no more hiding, no more chasing. Adam Hart is just a nightmare. Two weeks lost for me but nobody else will ever give a damn—because nobody else will ever know." His voice was thick. "Scott dead, Grossman dead, Van dead, Olson dead, Eddy dead. Nobody left alive but us."

The rain beat against his face and the water seeped down inside his collar and trickled down his neck. He felt cold and wet and sick and lonely.

Nordlund got out of the car. "Help me get him in the car, Marge, he's sick." He put his hand on Tanner's shoulder. Tanner knocked it away and backed off a step. The amusement park was empty now, the lights all out except for the headlights of the automobile. There was no sound except the thin mutter of music coming from the car radio and the steady rumble of thunder. They were alone in the amusement park.

Alone.

Nordlund was solicitous. "What's the matter, Bill?"

"I don't want to go with you."

"What the devil's eating you? Why not?"

Tanner backed away another step. It was too late to run, it was too late to hide, it was too late to pretend he didn't know. "I'm not going anyplace with you, Hart."

NORDLUND stared at him, his mouth open. "You're out of your mind, Professor."

Tanner's bowels had turned to water and he was afraid he was going to lose everything while he stood there. "Not yet," he chattered, "but I soon will be, won't I?"

Marge was very close to him, trying to put her arms around him. "Bill, you're sick. Come with us and we'll . . ."

He got the pistol out of his pocket and held it in a trembling hand. "Stay away, Marge. I know you're a puppet but I don't want to kill you. Stay away from me. *Please!*"

She hesitated and unwillingly let him go. Nordlund said, "I don't blame you for being frightened, Professor.

You've been through a lot. It's only natural that you should be close to cracking. But you've got to get a grip on yourself, man—you've got to pull yourself together!"

It sounded so plausible, so logical. He was worn out and tired and Nordlund only wanted to help. It would be so easy to lie to himself. . . .

Nordlund held the car door open. "Come on, get in and I'll drive you to a motel."

"Some drive." Tanner's voice was still shaking. "You and Marge and me, all alone. How many pieces would I get to the motel in? By the time you got through with me, I could be stuck in a letter and mailed there."

"I'm losing my temper," Nordlund said, his lips tight. "I almost lost my life, too, remember? And if it hadn't been for you, I would have died."

Tanner bobbed his head quickly. "Yeah, good act. One of the best I've ever seen. I believed it. But it was just an act. It would have been much more convincing if I had gone up earlier, though, wouldn't've it? But you had to string it out too long, you had to pretend that you had fought off Hart for half an hour. It can't be done. I know. *Nobody* can fight *you* off for that long—not the first time! And what would have happened if I had gone up alone?"

Nordlund shook his head pityingly. "You've really stripped your gears, Professor. You've really gone overboard."

"I really have, haven't I? But I think I stripped them long ago—I must have to have been so stupid. You were the most logical candidate all the time. The Navy man, slipping into survival research so you would know just how close anybody might be to tagging you, to guessing that there might be somebody like you. How many reports never got to Washington, how much information was misfiled? And what a spot for you! What an opportunity to meet important people and have easy access to classified files!"

The rain was cold and the wind was raw and he felt on fire with fever. He was going to come down with pneumonia, he thought—but that didn't matter a bit.

"And nobody had a photograph of you, Commander. Your yeoman showed me a picture one day and I'll bet he had a fatal heart attack that same afternoon, didn't he? A fuzzy photograph—the Navy doesn't have a clear one of you at all, does it? And nobody ever remembers to get one, do they?"

Nordlund tried to reason with him like he would with a small child. "Look, Professor, Adam Hart was just killed. You saw him back there, dead, just half an hour ago."

The thought of DeFalco sobered Tanner. "Poor Eddy. You were planning to use him from the very start, weren't you? And when it came time to stage your production number, you used him as bait. You pulled the strings and served him up on a silver platter. You made him pull the gun when he was about to leave at the exit, to make sure the police would kill him!" He paused, trying to control his voice. "I should have guessed—it was all so easy for me when Commander Nordlund started to help!"

"Do you think that everything DeFalco did was human?" Nordlund asked dryly. "Do you think a human being could have made it through the gunfire and leaped from beam to beam on the framework like he did?"

Tanner was half screaming now, the rain streaming down his face and running into his mouth and fuzzing his words. "Sure he could—with you pulling the strings! You! Sitting on the bench and pretending to be asleep! It took a lot of concentration to run him around, didn't it? You sat there and worked the wires and watched your puppet dance! And I'll bet it was goddamned difficult keeping him together for as long as you did, wasn't it?"

Nordlund shook his head sadly. Marge was crying.

Tanner felt hoarse. "DeFalco couldn't have been you, Adam! He died too easy and he died in a stupid way. You would have died hard and you would have been clever, you wouldn't have made any grandstand plays!"

He took a breath. There was no stopping now, he was committed. "I should have guessed Nordlund was you when you pulled the act in your way. You were after the rest of us because we were investigating him, because it wouldn't be long before we knew too much. Olson was killed because he could finger you, Van because he failed you, and Karl and Scott because they were too curious. And Eddy was your ace in the hole from the start, wasn't he? But there was absolutely no reason to kill 'Commander Nordlund.' He wasn't investigating, he wasn't even interested!

"And the main reason why Eddy couldn't have been you— the reason you overlooked because you didn't know about it. DeFalco had an opportunity to kill me once, in the cemetery after Olson's burial. There was nobody around, we were absolutely alone. It could have been done quickly and quietly and there were gravediggers behind the hill who could have hidden the evidence! If DeFalco had been you, he wouldn't have overlooked that chance!"

He was crying with exhaustion now and his voice came out in huge sobs. "I wanted out a dozen times, I wanted to forget all about it! Why did you keep hounding me, Hart? Why?"

He didn't wait for an answer but did what he had to do. He squeezed the trigger twice, before he could even think about it, then let his arm fall to his side and started backing away.

Both shots had missed. The man in front of him hadn't moved, except to turn up his raincoat collar against the driving wetness.

And then the picture was complete.

The night and the rain and the scudding clouds and the two of them. The belted Navy raincoat with the turned-up collar and the soft hat, dripping rain, that kept the face in shadow. Commander Arthur Nordlund.

The Enemy.

Adam Hart.

Tanner turned and ran and was almost to the funhouse entrance when something caught him and spun him around so hard he slipped to his knees on the walk. The man a hundred feet away still hadn't moved.

Olson.

Scott.

Grossman.

Van Zandt.

DeFalco.

you don't think you're going to get away, do you, animal?

The muscles in the soles of his feet suddenly knotted and cramped so hard it brought a shriek of pain to his lips. He didn't want to get up, he knew what torture it would be to stand on them. He wanted to lie in the mud at the side of the walk and die there, to lie on his stomach and breathe the ditch water and hope he drowned before Hart tore up his insides like he had the dog's.

He got to his feet.

He screamed with agony when he stood on them but he made it inside the grinning lips of the fun house door. Out of sight and the pressure was less and he started running down the tracks the little funhouse cars rode on. The cars themselves were outside, covered with canvas.

He glanced back once and saw a figure in the doorway and shot wildly at it, a fraction of a second before his arm developed cramps and his biceps felt like somebody had gripped them and was grinding in until sharp fingers touched the bone. He couldn't see in the darkness and he banged into the curving walls and felt the blood spurt from his nose.

don't run . . .

The whisper formed in his mind like a bubble of smoke. The gravel of the tracks seemed to grow to the size of rocks and he stumbled and fell and cut his knees. It was getting hard to breathe. The very air was viscous, like molasses. Funny. The laughter ripped from his throat. Like molasses.

don't run . . .

He didn't catch the faint flicking of the switch, the silent purr of the electrically operated machinery. He wasn't ready for it when he stumbled around a corner and the Laughing Lady swayed out from the wall, luminous and red-faced, big, puffy balloon arms holding her stomach as she rocked back and forth roaring with recorded laughter.

"Don't run! Ho-ho-ho-hah-hah-hah! Don't run! Hah-hah-hah! DON'T RUN! HO-HO-HO! DON'T RUN!"

The sound roared down at him and the balloon arms brushed him, thick rubbery fingers trailing across his face and shoulders. He screamed and fired at it and little cogs and wheels came spurting out and the big balloon arms sagged limply and the voice died in a gurgle. He was rushing down the tracks now, screaming frantically as the artificial spiderwebs brushed him or the dancing skeletons leaped out, their bony fingers stabbing at him and their voices shrieking.

It was only a low rumble that warned him in time. The low, rumbling sound and the slight quivering of the track. He flattened himself against the wall and the sound roared down at him, then the cars were rattling past, a bare two inches' clearance between himself and them.

Silent laughter bellowed through his mind like it must have bellowed through Van Zandt's before he had died. The laughter of a crazed thing that liked to see the animals die, whose final act for his puppets was always suicide.

There was a ledge paralleling the track and he climbed up on it. A passageway opened off of it and he ran through. He abruptly tripped and fell flat, angular boards cutting into his chest and stomach. A passageway with the tilt boards, like miniature teetertotters, that kept turning one way or the other. He got up and picked his way down the passageway, rounded another corner, and came out in a small, closed room with a red glow coming from a wall niche.

Satan in red, flames leaping at his feet, wearing the face of Arthur Nordlund. Only slightly twisted, slightly inhuman, and vastly . . . beautiful.

There was a noise behind him and Tanner whirled. The passageway he had come through was closed tight and he was locked in the room. He battered frantically at the walls and then another whirring sound started. The floor fell away from him and a side wall opened up and he found himself sliding down a strip of canvas with rollers beneath it.

The canvas was the tongue of the grinning exit-entrance and a moment later he was out in the open and the rain was washing over him. Full circle and he had come back to face the Enemy a hundred feet away.

There were little pricklings in his arms and legs and the nerves went to sleep. His fingers lost their power to grip and the pistol slipped from his hand to fall on the asphalt. The pressure on his mind was rubbing away his sense impressions of the world like he had seen old ladies rub out the wrinkles in their foreheads. There was a relaxation of his muscular sphincters and a loss of feeling and connection with his own body. He tried to fight it, to will himself to feel and hear and respond. He didn't succeed.

His legs gone and his arms numb and his pulse slowing and vague surprise that his breathing had stopped entirely. Then he was alone in the shadows of his mind, his consciousness dimming out like a spark that grows dimmer and dimmer until it's a tiny light and then a twinkle and then nothing at all.

The fading impressions of the night.

The rain.

The damp cold.

Then no night, no rain, no feeling, no impressions at all. Just the tiny coal in the huge wilderness of his own brain.

He didn't do it consciously and he did it without apparent effort. He reached out to Marge standing nearby. An overwhelming sense of empathy, a curious feeling of physical nearness, and a sudden brilliant pattern of tiny red threads that thinned out into nothingness. A feeling of resistance and an odd sensation of mixing . . .

The night and his impressions of it returned, but they were a different set of impressions this time. He had a different sense of being, and a vague cloud of emotions hampered his thinking. There was a different feeling to the air and the night and the rain. He realized he was seeing the world through different eyes—it was distorted and yet familiar.

He looked around and saw himself sinking to the shining black of the asphalt. A hundred feet away was the intense, glittering face of Adam Hart, the muscles in his face standing out rigid with the effort of his concentration.

It was like working a marionette. He pulled the strings and Marge responded.

She walked over and picked up the gun where he had dropped it. She turned and pointed it at Adam Hart. There was a flicker of awareness on Hart's part, then, and a sudden change of pressure. For a moment Tanner was receiving two sets of sense impressions, seeing the world as if it were on stereoscopic slides and his eyes hadn't quite meshed. Then Marge's sense impressions began to fade and he knew that if he didn't act now, Hart would be safe.

It took two shots to cut Adam Hart down.

Tanner stared at the body and watched the water run down the dead man's face and soak the clothes and collect in a puddle by the feet where the asphalt was a little lower. It still looked a little like Arthur Nordlund but the body was heavier and broader and the face was . . . handsome. The features were smooth and even, the mouth full and pouting. Somebody you would look at twice, somebody you would remember. Heterosis, Scott had written. Where two people of diverse racial stocks have children and the offspring retain all of the superior qualities of the parents and are superior to either.

Adam Hart.

The handsome gypsy boy from Brockton.

The man with the Power.

Dead. As dead as if he had been run over by a truck or knifed by thieves. Dead and all his dreams dead with him. But you couldn't judge him like you would anybody else, Tanner thought. It wouldn't be fair. He hadn't been human.

Then he wondered how long it had been since he and Adam had stood there and faced each other. Five minutes? Ten? The police would be arriving at any minute. Then they would ask him why he had shot Nordlund. He would tell them a monster had been killed and they would stare at him coldly and somebody would say, *"He's Commander Arthur Nordlund, Professor. I liked him a lot. I thought he was a very decent sort of human being."*

That's what they all would say, that's what. . . . But nobody would recognize the body on the ground as being Arthur Nordlund. Nobody would. . . .

No more running through the streets. No more hiding. The man with the Power was dead.

Dead.

Somebody was crying and he looked up. Marge stood a short distance away, sobbing softly. When she looked up at him the expression on her face was a curious mixture of loathing and repulsion and desire and awe.

Then he remembered *all* that had happened.

The committee meeting, so long ago. Somebody had moved the little paper umbrella. But if Hart had been the cautious type, would he have betrayed himself, even though Olson had thought he would? No. So somebody else must have moved it. He had gone all around the room. If somebody had had the Power and hadn't known it, they would have moved it then.

He had asked everybody to try but he hadn't tried it himself. Not until, to satisfy Olson, he had asked them all to try together. And then he himself had joined in and the little paper umbrella had obligingly moved.

He glanced back at the fun house. There was a small light bulb over the entrance and a loose, plastic shade on top. He stared at it and it moved slowly, then picked up speed.

Power, power, who had the Power?

He had.

And hadn't known it.

Hart must have known immediately who and what he was then. And Hart had tried to kill him. But he had survived. That should have been the tipoff. For two whole weeks, despite everything that Hart could do. Three times Hart had tried to kill him. And had failed each time.

And the last time Hart's pressure had finally primed the pump, had finally brought his own talents out into the open. Hart had probably been desperately afraid of that, but he had had to take the chance.

And there had been the clue of heterosis. The gypsy boy from Brockton, the far-superior offspring of mixed parentage. The one case where two and two had made five. And his own parents. The Santuccis on his mother's side and the Tanners on his father's. English and Italian. And his mother had been a sometime fortune teller and his father had foreseen the future when he had predicted his own death. They had had wild talents, talents they had passed on to him.

There had been other clues. The photographs for one. Hart had never taken a good photograph. And neither had he. The papers had never run one when he had been wanted for murder. They had never been able to find one that would have reproduced. And the photograph in the frame in Marge's room. Hart had used her but Hart had never given her a picture.

But *he* had.

The blank sheet of photographic paper in the frame had been a picture of himself.

Why had Hart tried so desperately to kill him?

He thought about it for a minute, and then he knew. Hart hadn't given a damn whether his own race procreated and grew and eventually replaced homo sapiens. He hadn't cared whether his own children had lived or died. He had gotten on the committee for the sole purpose of eliminating others like himself.

So he, Tanner, had had to die. And the others on the committee had been slated for death because they had discovered that a man like Adam Hart existed—and they could have spread the information. And who was to say that if there were others like Adam Hart, they might not have tried to kill Adam for the same reason Adam would have tried to kill them?

In Hart's mind, there had been room enough in the world for only one man with the Power.

It was funny, Tanner thought. Human beings, when they

thought of the superman, invariably gifted him with a super-human morality—the lust for personal power was not supposed to be one of his vices. But it hadn't applied to Adam Hart.

And it didn't apply to him.

He stood there in the darkness and shed his human identity like a snake shed its skin. He glanced at the animal that was crying a few feet away from him, then turned on his heel and strode towards the entrance, ignoring the wind and the rain and the exhaustion that had, after all, been only a *human* exhaustion.

Outside was the sleeping city, the lights glowing dimly in the shiny blackness. The lights that marched out from Chicago, down the highways and across the continents until they spanned the whole vast globe itself.

The thought occurred to him then, as it must have to Adam Hart years before.

It was going to be fun to play God.